"Bill, I'm not who you think I am," Delilah whispered.

"Didn't anyone ever tell you not to contradict a man who's kissing your neck?" he whispered back, moving his lips to her throat. When she shivered in sensual response, he drew back a fraction of an inch to stare into her eyes. "I know what you are. I know who you are. You're the melody that's been playing across the back of my mind for years. Elusive, haunting, and so incredibly beautiful."

She wasn't, but sweet heaven, she wished she were. At that moment she would have given anything to be the woman Bill thought she was.

What could it hurt to pretend a little longer? she asked herself. The deed was already done; a few minutes more couldn't possibly make any difference. For just a little while, she wanted to be someone special. . . .

WHAT ARE *LOVESWEPT* ROMANCES?

They are stories of true romance and touching emotion. We believe those two very important ingredients are constants in our highly sensual and very believable stories in the *LOVESWEPT* line. Our goal is to give you, the reader, stories of consistently high quality that may sometimes make you laugh, sometimes make you cry, but are always fresh and creative and contain many delightful surprises within their pages.

Most romance fans read an enormous number of books. Those they truly love, they keep. Others may be traded with friends and soon forgotten. We hope that each *LOVESWEPT* romance will be a treasure—a "keeper." We will always try to publish

LOVE STORIES YOU'LL NEVER FORGET
BY AUTHORS YOU'LL ALWAYS REMEMBER

The Editors

LOVESWEPT® • 329

Billie Green
Waiting for Lila

 BANTAM BOOKS
NEW YORK • TORONTO • LONDON • SYDNEY • AUCKLAND

WAITING FOR LILA
A Bantam Book / May 1989

If you would be interested in receiving protective vinyl
covers for your Loveswept books, please write to this address
for information:

Loveswept
Bantam Books
P.O. Box 985
Hicksville, NY 11802

ISBN 0-553-21956-1

Published simultaneously in the United States and Canada

Bantam Books are published by Bantam Books, a division
of Bantam Doubleday Dell Publishing Group, Inc. Its trademark, consisting of the words "Bantam Books" and the
portrayal of a rooster, is Registered in U.S. Patent and
Trademark Office and in other countries. Marca Registrada.
Bantam Books, 666 Fifth Avenue, New York, New York 10103.

To Pete and Sunny.
Welcome home.
Now Texas has everything.

One

In the aisle seat on the plane bound for Acapulco, Bill Shelley sat with his eyes closed, pretending to be asleep so he could escape the attention of Margo, the woman in the window seat. In the seat between them was That Poor Man, Margo's husband, Gerald.

Bill had listened to Margo complain from the minute they had left Houston, and now a headache was beginning to form behind his closed eyes. Shutting Margo out wasn't easy.

Suddenly, from somewhere ahead of him in the plane, Bill heard a woman laugh. Margo's voice faded, conquered by the soft sound of the incredible laughter. It wasn't the first time since leaving Houston that Bill had heard it, and, as before, it had the strangest effect on him. He could compare it only to someone taking a pillow and fluffing it into a more comfortable shape. That's what the laugh did to him. It knocked out all the lumps.

It fluffed him into shape, giving him more full-ness, more substance. More joy in just being alive.

He was tired, he told himself. He was overworked. He was going off the deep end because of exhaustion. *Fluff my heart and I'll follow you anywhere*, he thought wryly.

Opening his eyes a little, he began to scan the passengers in the aisle seats ahead of him. He was searching for The Laugh.

The redhead just in front and to his right? She was a small woman, and when she turned slightly to the man across the aisle, Bill saw a sweet, shy face. But it hadn't been a sweet, shy laugh.

Maybe it was the brunette two rows up. The back of her head looked elegant and regal, and the nape of her neck was definitely intriguing.

Just then the brunette raised a slender hand to hail a flight attendant. The gesture was haughty, imperious. The Laugh had been anything but haughty.

Two rows up from the brunette, blue-tinted hair sat next to short brown hair. He had taken a walk up the aisle earlier, and he knew the brown hair looked like a phys ed teacher. She certainly had an impressive build, and if she bench-pressed less than a hundred and fifty pounds, Bill would eat his hat.

No, he told himself, it wasn't a muscular laugh.

He remembered seeing two blondes sitting next to each other in the front of the plane. One had a platinum fall of hair that almost covered her shoulders. A fairy-tale princess, delicate and dreamy.

The other woman's hair was upswept and brushed with gold, as though Midas had passed a light, caressing hand across it.

Bill decided he would vote for one of the blondes. The Laugh probably belonged to the gym teacher or the blue-haired elderly woman, but since his imagination was free to go anywhere, he would pretend The Laugh came from a more attractive source.

At that moment Margo turned her head, and Bill got his eyes closed just in time. After a few minutes his pretense of sleep became a reality, and later he thought maybe he dreamed about golden-haired laughter.

Bill was still drowsy when he stepped from the plane and unprepared for the sunlight that hit him full in the face, blinding him with its brilliance. Seconds later, as the world began to come again into focus, he saw the purple mountains, close in the background, that provided a fitting backdrop for the flamboyant world at sea level.

He had forgotten how absurdly beautiful Acapulco was, its colors brighter, bolder, and more intense than anything found in Bill's native Houston. Smiling slightly, he moved down the steps and onto the tarmac.

At the gate just beyond a security barrier he had to maneuver around several people carrying placards. He wouldn't have given them more than a passing glance if Margo hadn't begun tugging urgently at his sleeve.

"Who is Delilah?" she whispered loudly.

Bill stopped walking and raised a brow in inquiry. "Delilah?"

"That's what it says on the signs." She nodded toward the placards. "She must have been on the plane with us, but I didn't see anyone famous, did you?"

He thought of The Laugh. He wouldn't have been at all surprised to learn the laugh had come from someone famous. "As a matter of fact—" he began.

"This makes me so mad," Margo interrupted as she punched her husband in the shoulder. "Gerald, why didn't you pay more attention? You know I wasn't wearing my glasses." Without giving Gerald a chance to answer, Margo continued. "Maybe she's a Mexican actress. Is Delilah a Mexican name? I thought it was something out of the Bible."

Bill smiled. "I think they've probably discovered the Bible in Mexico."

"Oh, of course," Margo said in sudden understanding. "Missionaries."

"Fourteenth-century missionaries," he agreed.

"I can't keep up with all these new religions. Moonies and Charismatics and . . . what are those hairy ones?"

"Hasidic Jews?"

"No, that's not the name." She turned to her husband. "Gerald, what do you call those people who hang around the airport? I can't figure out why they call them hairy when as far as I can tell they're all bald."

Ignoring her question, her husband began to look through the canvas bag he carried on his shoulder. "What did you do with my sunscreen?" Gerald's distinctive nasal whine was yet another of the reasons Bill had decided to nap on the plane. "I had everything in here just exactly the way I wanted it. I don't know why you have to mess with my stuff. Some people would call it an invasion of privacy, Margo. Some people wouldn't put up with it. You know what the sun does to my nose. I don't see why you can't just—"

Bill used Gerald's pitiful harangue to get away from the couple, but since they had the way forward blocked, he backtracked to try to go around them. As he moved past the sign-carrying group, Bill again became an unwilling intruder on a private conversation.

"Are you sure she's on this plane?" The speaker was a slender man with Oriental features who leaned close to an attractive woman with radiant black hair.

"I wrote it down, Jack. She's probably just hanging back until the aisles clear. You know Delilah. She doesn't wait in line for anything."

When the woman turned, Bill could see the sign resting on her shoulder. Written in crayon were the words DELILAH FOR EMPRESS.

Bill chuckled softly. Whoever the mysterious Delilah was, she had four devoted fans, devoted but slightly bizarre. Although he wasn't normally a celebrity watcher, they intrigued Bill enough to make him linger a few feet away.

Another member of the group, a large man with curly hair, horn-rimmed glasses, and who wore a banner across his ample chest, said, "Maybe Delilah decided not to come. Her fiancé—what's his name? He owns a radio station or something."

"Paul," one of the others volunteered.

The large man nodded. "That's it. Maybe Paul talked her into staying home. You can bet that when Delilah is my fiancé, I won't let her move two feet away from me."

The group reacted with laughter and hoots of derision, then the brunette spoke again. "Where have you been, for heaven's sake? Delilah broke off her engagement to Paul months ago. I can't believe you didn't see it in the newspaper. Paul told a gossip columnist that he was absolutely devastated and thinking of jumping off a bridge into the Trinity River—I always thought Paul was a little too intense—but when someone told him that he would end up with his head stuck in the mud because the Trinity is only about three feet deep under that bridge and most of that is slime, he decided to get drunk instead.

"For the last six or seven weeks," she continued, "she's been dating a banker named Hamilton Lindley Wharton the Third."

"Gadzooks," the large man said, rolling his eyes expressively. "What a mouthful. Have you seen him, Glory? Does he look anything like his name?"

The woman nodded, her deep blue eyes sparkling with laughter. "Yes, I'm afraid so. He's sweet, but terribly pompous until he gets around Delilah. Then he acts like a nervous puppy."

"Knowing Delilah, I'll bet she has him house-broken by now," said a petite woman, the fourth and last member of the group.

"For sweet Pete's sake, Gerald! You can wait just a little while to start your precious vacation."

Margo's piercing voice came from right behind Bill and harshly intruded on his leisurely bout of people watching. He glanced over his shoulder and found That Poor Man being hauled backward so that his wife could get a closer look at the group near the ramp.

"You never think of what I would like to do," Margo complained. "Do I ask for much? I wanted to go to Disney World for our vacation, but that wasn't good enough for you. It had to be Aca-pulco. Well, we're here now, so let me get what little enjoyment out of this trip I can."

At the exact moment Bill had made up his mind to leave before Margo spotted him, he heard an-other voice, one that made him forget all thoughts of escape.

"Why, what a surprise. Imagine finding a gath-ering of loyal fans here in the middle of nowhere."

This voice, unlike Margo's, was worth listening to. It was exactly like The Laugh.

Not satin, Bill thought, straining to hear. It was more like raw silk, smooth and husky at the same time. The mixture was unique, vital, and so in-credibly sensual his blood ran faster in a sponta-neous response.

If Delilah was the keeper of The Laugh, he thought, raising one thick brow, even her voice was worth waiting for.

Turning toward the source, he found that several other people had had the same idea and had moved between him and the plane, effectively blocking his view. He began to push his way through, unwilling for the moment to examine his growing need to see this stranger named Delilah.

Seconds later he did just that and found himself staring in open-mouthed pleasure. It was the Midas blonde. She was tall, slender, and beautifully put together. Not only her hair but every inch of her seemed to have been touched with gold. She was unconsciously sensual, consciously elegant. On her, the blue cotton of her shirtwaist dress looked as luxurious as the finest quality silk.

Bill whistled softly in stunned admiration. Delilah wasn't simply beautiful, she was something from out of a dream. She stood regally apart, surveying through the dark lenses of her sunglasses the four people who had been eagerly awaiting her arrival.

"You don't know how much your reception means to me," she said, and Bill thought he detected great amusement in her voice. "No matter how many wonderful things life has waiting for me in the future, I promise I'll never forget you. You, my most loyal supporters. You, the little people, the inconsequential people, the wretched flotsam and jetsam of society, the skim milk upon which the cream of the world rests."

When she lifted her nose just a fraction of an inch higher, the group broke into laughter and began to crowd around her. She immediately took off her glasses, revealing the golden-brown eyes Bill had more than half expected. He watched her intently as she hugged and laughed her way through the group.

A moment later a loud noise from the terminal caused her to look up. Her gaze skimmed past Bill. He was almost certain that she hadn't actually taken in his presence, but as her eyes met his, then moved on past, something happened to him, something even bigger than the fluffed-pillow feeling. It was as though, for just a fraction of a second, he had no control over his own limbs. He had taken two steps toward her before he remembered that they were strangers.

It was an honest-to-gosh Twilight Zone sensation, and Bill couldn't decide whether to laugh or get himself to the nearest psychiatrist.

Bill had known beautiful women in his life; he had even dated a few. So he knew it wasn't this woman's fantastic looks that caused him to react so strongly. That would have been a normal reaction, an ordinary reaction. What he was experiencing went way beyond ordinary.

In fact, he thought, it was damned spooky. Because, although he had never seen her before, when their eyes had met for that split second, there had been a moment of distinct recognition.

There had to be an explanation, he told himself, furrows of concentration appearing in his brow as he stared at her. He had never been given to quirky moods or flights of fancy, and the phenomenon known as precognition was a bit too equivocal for his taste.

Nevertheless, there had been something between them. Or at least something in him. But what was it?

After a moment his eyes widened in astonished understanding. He rubbed his chin, and a peculiar little smile twisted his lips as he shook his head and whispered, "Well, I'll be damned."

Two

Bill stood and watched, shamelessly eavesdropping as the beautiful Delilah let her friends crowd around her. He examined the expression on her face and knew without doubt that these people were important to her

"You said you'd never forget the little people." The large man leaned his head against Delilah's shoulder, gazing up at her with soulful brown eyes. "But you didn't say anything about me."

Bill swallowed a laugh when he saw that the man wore a white satin banner draped across his extra-wide chest. The words DELILAH'S DOMINANT DISCIPLE were written on it in neon pink marker.

"Booger darling"—the golden huskiness of her voice sank into Bill's flesh, all the way to the bones—"I've pined for you every minute we've been apart."

"Of course you have," the man called Booger

said solemnly. "A man of my magnitude isn't easy to forget."

"A man of your bulk isn't easy to forget," said the man with Oriental features. "Heaven knows I've tried often enough. Trash him, Delilah. Have a fling with a real man."

"I don't think so, Jack," Delilah said. Her tone of voice was serious, but her golden eyes sparkled with fun. "I couldn't stand breaking the hearts of the millions of shallow women who love you."

A short, slightly stocky woman rolled her eyes expressively behind the round frames of her thick glasses. "Can't you two think of anything except sex?"

"No," both men said simultaneously and emphatically.

"Pay no attention to them," the raven-haired woman said. "My theory is that the warm climate has made their brains swell, which is why Jack"— Bill assumed the man with Oriental features was Jack—"has been running around beating his chest and flexing his muscles, and Booger tries to convince every woman he sees to let him take her chest measurements—strictly in the interest of science, he says. Thank goodness Alan seems immune to whatever is in the air here."

"Speaking of your loving husband, where is he?" Delilah asked.

"He had business to take care of or he would have come to the airport with us," Glory explained.

"A likely story," Booger scoffed. "Doesn't it seem

a little strange that he remembered this 'business' the minute he saw our placards?"

Delilah grinned. "A prudent man is our Alan."

"An unmitigated coward is our Alan," Jack corrected her.

Glory raised one fist, shaking it at the group at large. "He's my honey and I'll defend his circumspection with my last breath. Besides, he's learning and growing every day. In fact, last week he played a practical joke on my father. He misquoted a stock report."

"There's a knee slapper if I ever heard one," the stocky woman said, crossing her eyes.

As they talked, they moved toward the airport terminal. Bill followed along behind them. He hadn't made a conscious decision to tag along. He simply seemed to have no choice.

At that moment a group of musicians pushed abruptly in front of him, and, since his gaze was on Delilah, Bill stumbled into one of the men, causing him to drop his instrument case. By the time Bill had apologized and helped the man, Delilah and her group had disappeared.

Glancing around, Bill shook his head. He was annoyed but not discouraged. He would find her. He was sure of it. Even though there were quite a few hotels in Acapulco, even though it might take all his spare time, one way or another he would find the golden girl.

Later, Bill's annoyance was tinged with just a little peevishness. His afternoon meeting had taken much longer than expected, so instead of searching for Delilah as he had planned to do, he now sat in the hotel's small bar, thinking about her.

La Porta, the hotel Bill had chosen, was not the most luxurious in Acapulco, but it suited him. A sprawling, palm-shaded structure, it was four stories tall and had pristine white walls as well as the obligatory red tile roof. It had seemed exactly right when he chose it, but now he wondered if he would have had a better chance of finding the glorious Delilah in one of the splashier hotels.

Then suddenly he heard The Laugh, and glancing up, he saw Delilah and her friends walk into the bar. They sat at a larger table approximately halfway across the small room from Bill. His luck had held.

"So that's why we're staying here," a stocky woman was saying. "And we were lucky to get a suite. Two small conferences are being held at La Porta this week."

"UPA and IJAMA," Booger said.

Delilah stared at him, one slender brow raised. "I know a speech therapist who can fix that problem."

"UPA is the United Plumbers Association and IJAMA stands for the Independent Jazz Artists of Mid-America," Booger explained. "Nice bunch of guys, but they don't need suites."

"Addie dear," Delilah said to the stocky woman, "I hope you've grown out of that tedious habit of—remove your hand from my thigh, Jack—leaving the light on all night long. I haven't had to wear a sleeping mask in the three years since we were roommates."

While Addie huffed, the rest of the group laughed good-naturedly. Obviously their friendship was well established.

"If she does," Glory said, "you won't be able to steal my bedroom this time, Dee."

"Not unless you have Alan's permission to share," Booger put in, then the large man groaned loudly. "Glory and Delilah together in the same bed—now, there's an idea that'll get the old hormones zipping along."

"Forget it," Glory said. "Alan might like it, but if he admits it, he's dead meat."

"I wouldn't stay up all night worrying about it," Delilah said, smiling slightly. "He doesn't know any other woman but you exists."

Bill didn't know what kind of man Glory's husband was, but unless he were made of stone, he had to be susceptible. No one could forget that Delilah existed.

"Okay," Jack said, grabbing Delilah's arm to get her attention. "Stop dillydallying around and tell us what happened to this Hamilton Langley Whitfield the Third."

She threw him an innocent look. "It's Hamilton *Lindley Wharton*, and there's nothing to tell. I'm afraid Ham didn't quite understand what I'm all about. In fact, it's only in this decade that his family has stopped thinking of professional people as hired help. Which is why he and I have agreed to sever our relationship."

Bill felt inordinately pleased that she was no longer tied to the man with the pompous name. And apparently her friends felt the same way. They all whooped loudly, then Booger began to chant, "And another one bites the dust. And another one bites the dust."

Delilah threw an ice cube at him. "Could you grant a dead relationship a little dignity, please?"

"I liked Ham," Glory said. "I wish I could understand what you're looking for, Dee. The last three men have all been spectacular."

"We discussed all this in the suite," Delilah said. "And just remember what I told you."

"I can't believe Booger even suggested it," Glory said, chuckling as she shook her head. "It finally happened. Einstein's brain has imploded."

"I really don't think I brought enough aspirin for this trip," Delilah said as she stared at the large man. "We should have had him committed years ago. Is it right to let him run loose in society simply because we're too sentimental to put him in a padded room?"

"I've been thinking about Booger's suggestion," Jack said, tapping his finger on his chin thoughtfully. "And I've come to the conclusion that we were too hasty. Although I hate to admit it, the cerebral psychopath might just be on to something this time." He paused, looking around at the others in the room. "We all need to make contacts— that's what we're here for, after all—so what's wrong with meeting a few new people?"

Bill leaned closer, even more intrigued than ever.

What were they up to, and why was Delilah looking as though she had slipped down the White Rabbit's hole?

Addie's thick glasses had slipped down on her diminutive nose as she carefully considered the mysterious proposition. "You know, this might work out."

"And the winner gets a prize," Booger said.

"That's it," Glory said as excitement grew in her brilliant blue eyes. "A prize."

"You traitors," Delilah muttered. She seemed to be torn between laughter and apprehension.

"What prize?" This was from Addie. "I want to know what the prize is before I waste my time looking."

"The winner gets to sleep with Delilah," Jack said, looking improbably innocent.

Glory shook her head doubtfully. "I don't think so."

"I've got it!" Addie's gray eyes were shining with greed. "The winner gets Dee's fox jacket."

"Naw," Jack said, "I don't have a thing to wear with it."

One by one they all turned to look at Booger. "Well, Mr. Wizard, what's the prize?" Jack asked.

Booger stared thoughtfully into space. After a moment a cherubic smile spread across his face. "The victor will be unanimously declared—once and for all, indisputably, now and in perpetuity— the most superior member of this group."

"Yes. Yes!" Jack said, raising a clenched fist. "I love it. At last each and every one of you will have to admit what I've been telling you for years: Jack Takara is the greatest."

"You've got the right idea," Booger said, smiling smugly. "Except for one small detail—the name of the winner. And when I win, I'll expect proper obeisance from everyone, especially the women."

Delilah tapped on her glass with a spoon. When she had the group's attention, she looked at them with narrowed eyes. "I want it clearly understood that I do not condone this lunacy. I know you people too well. My name and measurements will be on the bulletin board in the lobby and in telephone booths and on the walls in the men's rooms."

Addie snapped her fingers. "The bulletin board! I had already thought of the telephone booth and the men's rooms, but not the—"

Delilah rolled her eyes. "You see what I mean?"

Glory laughed. "Relax. I promise we'll be discreet. No one will throw your name around. Come on, Dee, be a sport."

Delilah stared at her for a moment, then sighed. "I must be out of my mind."

"That's okay. We still love you," Jack said as he stood and began to move toward the entrance to the bar.

Booger jumped up and shouldered Jack roughly out of the way, shouting, "Let the games begin!"

"Total idiots," Addie muttered.

"But cute," Glory added. "I have a feeling this is going to be an interesting week." She glanced at Delilah, then shook her head. "I don't suppose I'll ever understand you, but I hope you get what you want."

Addie sighed. "I hope we all get what we want on this trip." She glanced at Glory. "Including you. Is something wrong? You look a little tired— no, not tired exactly, distracted and . . . sad? Are you sad, Glory?"

Bill blinked when he saw Delilah's instant alertness. He knew suddenly that Glory was someone special to his golden girl.

"Sad?" Glory echoed with a short laugh. "What on earth would I have to be sad about? I have a wonderful husband, the kind of man women fight over. I'm in sunny Acapulco with the strangest but best friends in the world. And to top it off"— she rose to her feet—"I will soon be the undisputed superior member of the group." She grinned. "Because I'm going to win."

At the entrance to the bar she glanced over her shoulder at Delilah and Addie. "To the hunt!"

After a moment Addie gave Delilah a puzzled glance, then shrugged. "To the hunt," she said as she followed Glory out of the room.

Now was the time for Bill to make his move. He stood up and walked toward Delilah, then suddenly the same group of musicians he had seen at the airport walked into the bar and one of them recognized Bill.

By the time Bill politely explained he really didn't want them to buy him a drink, Delilah had disappeared.

"Damn, damn, *damn*," he said, then let out a

long breath. It was okay, he told himself. She was staying at the same hotel. The gods were with him.

Several hours later, when the sun hung low in the west, Bill stooped awkwardly on the red brick terrace of the hotel, shifting his position slightly to get the cramp out of his right leg. Beside him were a cheerful-looking dark-skinned boy and a sad-looking blue bicycle.

Shade for the trio was provided by a cluster of palm trees that grew right to the edge of the hotel terrace. Beyond the trees was a startlingly white stretch of beach. On the beach there were splashes of color in the form of blankets and bikinis. On the blankets and in the bikinis were the sun worshippers; old and young alike were uniformly brown and slick with tanning oil. Beyond the sun worshippers, dazzlingly blue water met dazzlingly blue sky.

"Tell you what, sport," Bill said to the boy, "I'm not an expert, but I believe we're going to need at least a pair of pliers to get this thing back together."

The boy scrambled to his feet. "I'll get some pliers quick. No one runs faster than Luis." The last words were said over his shoulder as he ran toward a row of buildings.

Bill smiled as he watched the boy disappear. Luis, an enterprising young man of about eight, hadn't been shy in asking for Bill's help with the bicycle, and Bill hadn't had the heart to tell the boy that he didn't know a thing about bicycles . . . or anything else mechanical for that matter.

For a reason heaven only knew, mechanical ability had been left out of Bill's genetic makeup, a fact that had caused him not a little embarrassment during his teenage years when his brothers and friends had spent ninety percent of their lives under the hoods of their cars.

Everyone who knew Bill understood that he was helpless in the face of gears and sprockets and moving parts, but Luis was still young enough to believe that adults were all-knowing simply because they were adults. Rather than disillusion him, Bill had decided it wouldn't hurt to give it a try. Maybe he was just a late bloomer.

"It won't work that way. You're trying to put it on backward."

Bill recognized the smooth, husky tones instantly, but even if he hadn't, he would have known it was Delilah by the way his heart, not to mention other parts of his body, reacted.

Glancing up, he found her standing beside him. Delectable Delilah, he thought with pleasure. The golden girl. Her hair was in one long braid that fell across her shoulder, and she now wore a black off-the-shoulder blouse and a wide silver belt with a hand-painted Mexican circle skirt and black sandals.

The look suited her, he decided. She had become a Gypsy with golden-blond hair. A seductive angel.

My angel, he told himself. That was the stunning truth that had hit him at the airport, the truth that had made him determined to find her, the truth that had made him shamelessly invade her privacy. This was his woman. This was the woman who had been made only for him.

He would have to go slowly, he told himself. He couldn't take a chance on scaring her off. He would have to be cautious and wait before he told her that she was the woman he had been looking for all his life, the woman he had feared didn't exist.

Yes, he told himself as he stared up at her with a totally captivated smile, he'd wait. He'd wait at least until tonight to ask her to marry him.

After a moment she shook her head, as though to clear it, and frowned. "Do I know you? Wait, I saw you in the bar. You were staring at Booger."

"Booger?" He rose to his feet but couldn't manage to take his gaze from her face.

"My large, slightly warped friend."

Bill remembered the man, but it hadn't been Booger who had caused him to stare. It was Delilah who had held his attention then, as she did now. And he had been thanking whatever guardian angel had been responsible for putting her in the same hotel with him, just as he was thanking it now.

"I apologize for staring. I'm Bill Shelley. And you're"—he smiled slowly, with real pleasure—"Delilah."

"How did you—oh, yes, the banner." Laughing, she extended her hand. "Delilah Jones."

He wiped his right hand on his khaki shorts and, in what seemed like slow motion, took hers. A remnant of sanity told him that shaking hands was an ordinary social ritual, but the remnant faded completely as the extraordinary pleasure of touching her took over. It required a genuine effort on his part to release her hand.

With a slightly puzzled expression she returned his stare, then said, "Did your chain slip off?"

"I wouldn't be surprised," he said. Then, "Oh, you mean the bicycle. It's Luis's bike and his chain." He grinned. "He seemed to think I could fix it."

"Luis?"

"A young friend I've just met. I sent him to get a pair of pliers."

"That's not necessary. Let me show you." She squatted beside the bicycle, then glanced up at him. "You're obviously not a plumber."

Bill laughed and stooped beside her, more fascinated than ever. "It's not how people usually start conversations with me, but I guess it's as good as anything else. Why can't I be a plumber?"

"I don't want to hurt your feelings, but you have no mechanical aptitude."

"I see what you mean. That's too bad. I hear plumbers make good money."

She reached across the bike to lift the chain. "Jazz musicians don't do so badly either, if they're good, that is."

"I suppose you're right." Bill had no idea what she was talking about, but it didn't bother him. She could recite Jabberwocky backward for all he cared, just as long as she kept talking, just as long as she stayed near.

"Are you good?"

With some women Bill would have taken the question as a not-too-subtle come-on, but not with this woman. There was genuine curiosity in the appraising look she gave him.

"Define 'good,' " he said cautiously.

"Do you play a musical instrument well enough to give others pleasure?"

"No, I'm afraid not," he admitted.

"Then maybe you should consider changing your profession," she suggested kindly.

"Believe me, I've considered it . . . often. But I can't. It has me hooked."

She nodded in sympathy. "I know exactly what you mean. Here, hold the bike up a little while I turn the pedal," she said, then glanced up as Luis returned with the pliers.

"The bicycle is mended?" the boy asked.

"Not yet, but now I have expert help." He saw the boy look longingly toward the beach and said, "Go ahead, play with your friends. I'll call you when Lila and I are through."

"*Gracias*, Bill . . . Lila," he said even as he turned toward the beach.

When Bill turned back to the woman beside him, he was struck by a strange expression on her beautiful face. Hers was an almost painfully wistful look, and it disturbed him deeply.

"What is it?" he said sharply.

"You called me Lila."

He frowned. "I'm sorry. It seemed to fit." The truth was, Lila sounded more intimate than

Delilah, and above all else Bill wanted to be on an intimate level with this woman. "Would you rather I didn't?"

"I don't know. No one except—no one calls me Lila now." She shook her head. "No, I don't mind." She sounded surprised, then almost relieved as she smiled at him. "I don't mind at all."

"Delilah!"

They both glanced up at the sound of her shouted name, then watched as two men approached. Bill recognized the slender man with Oriental features as Jack. The other was a stranger, a tall, angular man who looked confused and uncomfortable, as though he didn't quite know what he was doing there.

When the men reached them, Delilah rose slowly to her feet. "Bill, this is Jack Takara and . . ."

"And this is Frank Devlyn," Jack said, his voice hearty and portentous.

"Nice to meet you both." Bill reached out to shake hands with the men.

There was an awkward silence, then Jack said, "Well, I guess we'll let you get on with your repairs." His voice wasn't quite so hearty as he turned to Frank. "I'll catch up with you in the bar."

As soon as Frank was out of sight, Jack glanced at Delilah. "What's this? I don't get it. If I were a woman, I'd be drooling all over the place. He's exactly the kind of man I would choose for—"

"Jack darling." Delilah patted him on the shoulder. "Think about that statement, then get back to me."

Jack glanced at Bill. "I'm not positive, but I think I've just been insulted." He gave them both a good-natured grin and saluted. "I adjust."

As Jack walked away, Delilah stooped again beside the bicycle without offering a word of explanation. Bill stood for a moment, looking down at her, then a slow smile spread across his face.

He wanted to laugh out loud at the wonder of her. She was a pirate's cache. And he was going to have the time of his life sorting through the treasure.

Three

As Delilah worked on the bicycle, she openly studied the man beside her. He was of average height and weight, and his thick brown hair was the kind that looked habitually tousled and was a perfect match for his slightly crooked front teeth. He had the offbeat, carefree look of an adventurer.

She had noticed his blue-gray eyes in the bar, but now, as he glanced at her, she saw that his left eye was not completely blue-gray like the right one. One small section of the left eye was distinctly, brightly, green. It made her want to laugh in surprise and delight.

Cute. Definitely cute, she thought. But why was he smiling in that peculiar moonstruck way?

"By George, I think we've got it," Bill said, turning the pedal smoothly. Then he looked at her and grinned. "At least, I think you've got it. I would never have managed to fix it by myself."

"No," she agreed without inflection. "You wouldn't have."

He laughed, then stood and waved toward a group of boys on the beach. "Luis! The bicycle's ready."

Minutes later, after the boy and his friends had collected the bicycle and disappeared, Bill wiped his hands on a handkerchief as he stood smiling at Delilah.

"Lovely Lila to the rescue," he said. Taking her arm, he began to walk away from the terrace. "You've saved my reputation in Acapulco. I can hold my head high and not be afraid that people are snickering and making rude comments about me behind my back."

She laughed. "I suppose that's important, especially here in Mexico, the birthplace of machismo."

"The word may have come from Mexico, but I'm afraid the concept is universal. The majority of the men in the world, no matter what their nationality, waste big pieces of their lives trying to convince themselves that they are *real* men, whatever that means."

"You too?" She studied his features, her curiosity genuine.

"I'm afraid so," he admitted ruefully. "I tell myself I'm not as bad as a lot of men, but today, when I stepped off the plane . . . You see, I live in Houston, a nice city, but there is a sameness about big cities that makes them almost invisible to the people who spend their lives there. Acapulco is blinding in contrast. And a couple of hours ago, when I saw those again"—he gestured toward the mountains that rose on their left—"I felt the same thing I always feel."

"Small?" she ventured. "Helpless?"

He shook his head in a wry, negative movement. "No, I felt uncomfortable . . . embarrassed."

She stopped walking, her expression puzzled. "Why on earth would you feel embarrassed?"

"Because beauty so intense"—his gaze moved slowly over her face—"is a real problem for a man to deal with. It brings all the passions too close to the surface for comfort. A real man isn't supposed to get a lump in his throat simply because the world is suddenly a lovely place."

Delilah fell silent. There was much more to this man than she had supposed. She had been thinking of him as an attractive but ordinary man, the kind of thoroughly nice man found at Little League baseball games and church picnics. The kind of man Delilah had always been curious about but rarely came into contact with socially.

She glanced up and realized that they had left the row of hotels far behind. Why was she here, she wondered suddenly. She should be using every spare minute to accomplish the goal she had set for herself. She shouldn't be strolling along the beach with a self-admitted second-rate jazz musician.

It was that damn smile, she told herself. It was like a campfire on a chilly morning—one automatically tried to get closer to the warmth. And maybe part of the blame belonged to his crazy patchwork-quilt eyes. They were the eyes of a child, a little vulnerable, a little wistful, but always prepared for wonder and delight.

Yes, she thought with a frown, there was definitely more to Bill Shelley than what was on the surface. But why on earth should that disturb her?

As they walked, Delilah had been unconsciously listening to him whistle under his breath, and now something began to nag at her. "I know you said you weren't very good," she said slowly, "but what kind of musician can't carry a decent tune? That's not even jazz. It's—"

"Waylon Jennings."

She stared at his smile. "You're not a musician."

"Nope."

"Then you picked a really lousy time to vacation in Acapulco," she said, her tone admonishing. "The hotels are packed with conventioners. Why didn't you check, then put off your vacation until a better time?"

"Actually, I knew."

She raised one brow. "You must really like people."

He laughed softly. "Why do I feel I should apologize for that?"

"I haven't a clue," she said with a shrug. "It's no skin off my nose if you want to wade through miles of perspiring tourists on your vacation."

Judging by the quality of his clothes—and Delilah was a very good judge of quality—he could probably afford to come only at a time when cheap packages were available.

"So you're not a musician," she said. "What *do* you do for a living?"

He was silent for a long moment. "I don't think I want to tell you."

"Why not? Are you a gangster? A porno star?"

"Nothing so exciting," he said, laughing. "Haven't you ever noticed how you . . . how we all size people up at the first meeting? First we look at their clothes and check their jewelry, trying to guess how much it cost. We see if their nails are professionally manicured, whether their hair was cut by a barber or an expensive stylist. Then for the clincher we ask what their line of work is. We use all that information to make a judgment of some kind."

"What's wrong with that?" she asked, trying not to sound defensive. She didn't like knowing her previous thoughts had been so predictable.

"It gets in the way. Your opinion of a person is, quite naturally, colored by extraneous things."

She frowned, considering his theory. "I don't think I would call my profession an extraneous thing. It's too much a part of me."

"A part of you," he agreed. "But it isn't you." He paused. "I know a man, a perfectly obnoxious man, who didn't have a friend in the world until he wrote a screenplay that became a hit movie. Now everyone thinks he's wonderful. They don't seem to notice that he's even more obnoxious than he was before. Even I, knowing how thoroughly unpleasant he is, wonder at times if there's more to him than I think, simply because of what he does for a living."

She could see his point, but she had never regarded the human trait of sizing people up by their professions as a bad one. She liked the way people looked at her with respect when they found out she was a doctor. It put her on equal footing with anyone she met, and she wasn't sure she wanted to be without that advantage.

Don't be silly, she told herself. With or without the letters after her name, she was somebody. Why not play his little game? It might be fun to pretend to be an ordinary woman. A woman with no traumas in her past. A woman with no dark spots in her history.

Suddenly an unfamiliar yearning began to grow inside her. Compared to herself, Bill was almost an innocent. Just for a little while, why shouldn't she find out what it was like to be a normal woman having a lighthearted flirtation? It was the kind of thing that had been denied her in the past and would most certainly be denied her in the future.

She could pretend she was an ordinary woman with a loving family background. She could pretend that the world was a warm, pleasant place, and she was a warm, pleasant woman with nothing more on her mind than meeting a warm, pleasant man who might, in the future, be the center of her warm, pleasant life and father to her warm, pleasant children.

What a kick, she thought, her smile wistful. For today she would leave the image of hard-nosed, hard-hearted Delilah behind and see what the world was like for the women she had envied all her life.

"Let's do it," she said, unable to keep a note of excitement out of her voice. "For now we have no occupations. We'll be two unemployed individuals." She kicked up a spray of sand as she swung around to face him, walking backward as she spoke. "We'll be beach bums. I think I would make a sensational beach bum, don't you?"

He laughed, then picked up her hand to swing it between them. "Indubitably."

"Do beach bums say indubitably?"

"The ones with style do."

She liked him. This new, *nice* Delilah liked him a lot. It might just turn out to be a very interesting evening.

She glanced up at the mountains. "I didn't expect the mountains. They're wonderful. You said you've been here before. Tell me about them."

"They're the Sierra Madre del Sur. That's about all I can tell you, except that there's a village, Nuevo Oviedo, up there that's very special to me. It's about two hours from here and is one of the most beautiful places I've ever seen. Generally, in Mexico, when people say unspoiled they mean cruelly poor, but Nuevo Oviedo is different. There's an old-world atmosphere about the place, and although its people are not wealthy, you see real pride in their faces. In the United States the town we live in is simply a place we got transferred to or a place we decided to move to because there are job opportunities and good schools for our kids. To the people of Nuevo Oviedo, their village is an integral part of their lives. Not only do they consider the other residents a kind of extended family, the village itself—the buildings and the earth under their feet—is a part of them."

He paused, staring up at the mountains. "The head man of the village, Tomás Fuentes, is a remarkable man. He studies each child who is born in the village. He watches that child throughout his childhood, then he decides what occupation is best for the child and best for the village."

"You mean they have no say in the matter? That's . . . that's barbaric."

He laughed. "You'd have to meet him to understand. What he does wouldn't be possible in North America, but for Nuevo Oviedo it works." He stopped walking suddenly and turned to look at her. "I'm driving up there tomorrow. Why don't you come with me and see for yourself?"

Tomorrow the game would be over, she thought. Tomorrow hard-hearted Delilah would be back on track. She shook her head slowly. "I sorry but I can't. I'm with friends, and they have plans for tomorrow."

"That's too bad." His disappointment sounded genuine. "Are they good friends?"

"They are the people who mean more to me than anything else in the world," she said quietly. Then suddenly she remembered the game of pretense she had entered into. "Except for my family, of course. I'm afraid I take my family too much for granted. That's what they get for spoiling me."

"I know what you mean," he said, smiling. "Every once in a while it will suddenly hit me how terrific my family is—I have three sisters and two brothers—and how lucky I am to have them all. But most of the time I ride comfortably along, cheerfully assuming that they'll always be there when I need them."

She nodded knowingly. "I suppose your mother, like mine, slips you extra money every time you visit because she's positive you're starving to death. And Dad. The man amazes me. He'll call me about once a week and spend half an hour growling and grumbling about something I've done that he doesn't approve of. I always think I'm being cagey, simply making repentant noises, then when I hang up I realize he's somehow managed to get information out of me concerning every aspect of my life, including how much money I have in my savings account." She almost laughed at how easy she was finding it to plagiarize Addie's life. "I remember once—"

"Delilah!"

She broke off and, turning, she saw Booger walking quickly along the beach, dragging an apparently reluctant man behind him. When she and Bill stopped walking, Booger left the man and ran toward them. By the time he reached them he was panting hard. He bent over, placing his hands on his knees, his head down as he tried to catch his breath.

After a moment Delilah said, "Bill, this is Arnold Schlumburger."

Booger lifted one hand in a halfhearted acknowledgment, then, drawing in a deep, wheezing breath, he looked at Delilah and gestured toward the man he had left behind. "Well, what do you think?"

Delilah looked at the man, smiled brilliantly, then said in a low voice, "Booger, my one and only love, the man is wearing red socks."

"What?" He glanced at the man. "Yeah, you're right. I didn't notice."

"That's because you're also wearing red socks," she told him with compassion.

He dropped his gaze to his feet. "Son of a gun, so I am." He grinned sheepishly. "Oh, well, as the Three Stooges, those masters of inverted irony, said, 'If at first you don't succeed, keep on sucking till you do suck seed.' "

When he walked away, Delilah turned back to Bill. "Where was I? Oh, yes, my father."

Bill, still staring after Booger, opened his mouth to speak, then changed his mind and simply shook his head.

"One time," Delilah said, returning to the borrowed background, "my father somehow found out—don't ask me how; the man is omniscient—that I had cashed in one of my savings bonds because I needed extra money. For my next birthday, along with a gift from both of them, which my mother always buys, was not one but two savings bonds to replace the one I had redeemed. Do you believe it? He pretends I'm an adult with sense enough to make my own decisions, but he's always doing crazy things like that."

Bill smiled. "You don't sound too upset about his interference."

"He's an old poot," she said, copying the indulgent note she had often heard in Addie's voice when she spoke of her father.

"All fathers are old poots. It's some kind of rule. They have to take a test before they're allowed to bring the kid home from the hospital. My mother waits on my father hand and foot. Everything centers around him. And he never says one word of thanks, but I have a feeling something goes on between them when they're alone." He smiled. "There's a look in Mom's eyes when Dad's in the room. It's not adoration or worship; those things are more or less blind. It's some kind of knowledge, as though she knows all his weaknesses and they're part of why she loves him. That kind of thing makes for a secure childhood." He glanced at her. "You and I are lucky."

She avoided his gaze. "Yes," she said softly, "we were lucky to have had that kind of childhood."

"Enough," he said with a laugh. "Any more of this and I'll start feeling guilty about not calling my parents as often as I should."

"Do they live in Houston too?"

He shook his head. "They moved to a suburb of

Phoenix when Dad retired. My brothers and sisters are scattered all over the rest of the country."

As he related the horrors of his monthly telephone bill, Delilah carefully observed his animated features. She couldn't remember ever having had a casual conversation with a man before now. In the past she had always been planning what her next move would be, deciding what she could say and do to achieve whatever goal was uppermost in her mind at the time. This was totally different. With Bill she felt a freedom that was strangely exhilarating.

As they talked they began to walk back toward the hotel. When they drew near the terrace, Addie suddenly appeared. She grabbed Delilah's arm and nodded toward a man who stood with several other people near the swimming pool.

"Him," Addie said bluntly.

Before Delilah could open her mouth, Bill said, "He's too short."

"No, he's—" Addie dropped Delilah's arm and stared at Bill, her brow creasing in doubt. "Do you think so?"

"There's no doubt about it," Bill said flatly. "I'd say he's a good three inches too short. Lila would never be able to wear heels."

Addie sighed. "I guess you're right. I didn't think of that. He looked tall to me."

"That's because you're so adorably petite. I could pick you up and put you in my pocket."

Delilah said, "Addie Howard meet Bill Shelley."

"Hello, Addie," Bill said, smiling.

"Adorably petite?" she said without acknowledging the introduction. "I like that. And I like you. I might just want to climb into your pocket."

When he laughed, Addie glanced at Delilah, obviously gauging her five-seven height. "Look for a giant," she muttered, then walked away.

After a moment Bill rested his hands lightly on Delilah's bare shoulders. "I know a café that serves the best arroz con pollo in the civilized world. Will you share some with me? It's well away from the tourist traps as well as from matchmaking friends."

She laughed. "How did you know?"

"I'm afraid I listened in the bar. Plus I have too many friends of my own who have made it their life's work to 'find a nice girl for Bill.' "

She frowned. "How much did you hear?"

"Only that whoever finds you a date gets some kind of prize."

A date. Then he hadn't heard it all. He didn't know the real purpose of the search. Suddenly Delilah was glad. She didn't want him to be a part of her real life. She didn't want him to know about all the doubts, all the fears that had been behind the decision she had made before she flew to Acapulco.

Delilah never did anything on the spur of the moment. She looked at every detail and considered every possibility before making even the most minor decision. But now, with Bill, she didn't even stop to worry about the reason that without hesitation she said, "Let's go."

· · ·

The café was not at all what Delilah had expected. It was a busy little place, friendly and noisy, but there wasn't a piñata or a brightly painted pot in sight. Nets and harpoons decorated the unpainted wooden walls, making it look more like a fish and chips place from back home than a Mexican restaurant.

After they had given their orders to a young waitress, Delilah glanced up to find Bill watching her intently. "What?" she asked with a tiny, self-conscious smile. "Why are you staring at me like that?"

"I can't seem to do anything else. Haven't you noticed?" There wasn't a hint of apology in his voice. "I've been staring at you since the first time I saw you at the airport. Not just because you're beautiful, although heaven knows that's reason enough."

Bill leaned forward, eager for her to understand. He knew she must be used to men staring at her, men who were drawn to her looks but didn't care about the woman. He didn't want her to think he was the same. He didn't want her to think what was between them was the same.

"It's more," he continued. "It's something in your eyes, in your face. This is going to sound really foolish, but I recognized you."

She frowned slightly. "We're both from Texas. It's not impossible that we would have run across each other at some time in the past."

He shook his head emphatically. "No, I had never

seen you before you stepped off the plane, but I recognized you. I told you it would seem foolish."

"Yes," she agreed, her voice more wary than she had expected it to sound. "It seems foolish."

Delilah glanced away from the sincerity of his expression. Earlier she had had the same feeling he had described, a feeling of familiarity, but she had ignored it, unwilling to place any undue importance on it. Déjà vu happened every day, she told herself. There was nothing extraordinary about it. And fairy tales were for other people, not for Delilah Jones.

The silence at the table grew heavy for just a moment, then Bill smiled and said, "So tell me, how did you get to be Lila? Did you become you intentionally or did circumstances make you who you are?"

She shrugged. "Both, I guess. When I was fourteen I decided that I would control my own life, but circumstances caused me to make the decision."

She smiled wryly. Circumstance seemed such an innocuous word. Too mild for the events that had shaped her life and character.

"Fourteen seems a little young to make life decisions. You must have been very mature for your age."

Although his words weren't phrased as a question, she knew he wanted to know more. Her mouth went dry as she searched for something to say. The lies had come so easily on the beach. But suddenly, because he was who he was, she didn't want to lie to him.

But she also couldn't bear the thought of telling him the truth. She didn't want this nice man to find out who and what she really was. Not yet. She wanted the pretense to continue for just a little while longer.

"I guess I was mature," she began hesitantly, choosing her words with care. "I had to be. It started when Buddy—Buddy was my brother. He was the most terrific kid." She glanced up. "You would have liked him. He called me Lila too." She smiled at the memory. "He thought I was perfect. I remember taking him to his first day at school."

"You took him? Where was your mother?"

Delilah took a sip of wine to buy time. "Mama? Oh, she was there, but she was terribly indulgent. She knew I had my heart set on taking him, and she—well, she knew it would make me feel like an adult. I was ten then. Looking back, I can see that it must have been a great sacrifice on her part. She let me do everything for him that morning. I scrubbed him until he was shiny and dressed him, and—" She broke off and laughed. "He had this crazy little cowlick right at the front of his head. I sprayed it and sprayed it with hair spray— it's a wonder I didn't asphyxiate us both—but it kept bouncing right back." She shook her head. "I was more scared than he was that day. I didn't want to leave him with all those strangers. What if he needed me? I knew the teachers wouldn't let me leave class to go to him. You see, because he loved me so much, Buddy was my responsibility—"

She broke off and stared at her wineglass. "He died two days after my twelfth birthday."

Bill had to check an impulse to pull her into his arms. For a moment she had looked like the devastated little girl she must have been when her brother died. But that wasn't all. Something more than an old tragedy was hurting her, hurting her badly, and Bill couldn't stand it. He wanted to hold her and make it all better. Never before had he felt so acutely pain that wasn't his own. But then, he thought, maybe it was his own.

Delilah was shocked that she had told this man so much. No one, no one on earth, knew so much about her. It had started with lies, but somewhere along the way it had turned into the truth.

Why, she asked herself. Why, when she had taken care all her adult life to never talk about her past, not even with the group, her special friends, should she suddenly tell so much to a man she had just met?

The explanation must rest in the fact that he was a stranger, a stranger she would never see again when she left Mexico. It had nothing to do with that feeling of recognition, she told herself firmly. Nothing.

When she felt his hand cover hers, she glanced up and was instantly taken aback by the depth of emotion that lay unconcealed in his eyes. It wasn't pity. She would have hated that. It was understanding. It was an unspoken offer to share her pain.

"I guess your brother's death is part of the reason you're so precious to your parents," he said slowly. "I don't blame your father and mother for trying to pamper you."

Delilah was suddenly tired of the loving parents she had built for herself. She didn't need them. She had never needed them.

"Enough about family," she said, unable to keep a touch of harshness from her voice. "When you're not pretending to be a bicycle mechanic, what do you do for fun?"

As though he sensed her need to lighten the conversation, Bill began to tell her about his extracurricular activities, from sculpting to soccer to sailing. As the meal progressed, she became more and more relaxed, soothed by the warmth of his personality.

"I remember that concert," she said, laughing as a rock concert she had attended brought back memories. "Glory and I were dying to go, but money was scarce back then, back when we were in—" She broke off and shook her head. She had almost mentioned medical school. "I don't think I'd better finish that story. I almost gave the game away."

He studied her face, then smiled slowly. "Why don't we make this more interesting? The first one to mention his or her profession has to pay a penalty."

The lighthearted, flirtatious note in his voice sounded innocent enough, but she threw him a suspicious look. "What kind of penalty?"

"Something absolutely harmless." He didn't

sound quite so innocent now. "If I win, I get to kiss you. If you win, you get to kiss me. Nothing could be fairer than that."

She laughed, but inside her head alarm bells were going off. The past had developed in Delilah a keen instinct for self-preservation, the same instinct that was telling her now that things between her and Bill were not quite as casual as she had thought.

In fact, she had the distinct feeling that kissing this man, instead of being absolutely harmless, might be very dangerous indeed.

Four

The night was as soft as velvet. Silver waves slid gently across the sand, and a salty breeze whispered through the palms, blending with the music from a distant mariachi band. Delilah and Bill walked hand in hand along the deserted beach toward the cluster of hotels, talking quietly as the night sounds played in the background.

"What does this remind you of?" Bill asked.

"This, the sand and water and sky? Or this, the tickling thing you're doing to my hand?"

"All of that. The night and us, what does it remind you of?"

She thought for a moment. "It reminds me of sand and water and sky and you doing tickling things to my hand."

"Boo, hiss. What are you, some kind of Scrooge? It's as plain as the nose on your face. This is Camelot."

"This is Acapulco, and my nose has never in its

life been plain," she said flatly. "I've been told more times than I can count that it's elegant."

"All right, it's as elegant as the nose on your face that this is Camelot."

"It's Camelot?" she asked with a sly smile.

"It's Camelot."

"Then dive into the water and bring me Excalibur."

He shook his head sadly. "You have to have something you can hold in your hand before you'll believe? All you have to do is listen to the magic. Hear that? That's Merlin telling you to wise up."

"Merlin?" she asked skeptically. "It sounded more like crickets to me. But I'll take your word for it. Although I suspect that maybe a few teeth have worn off your gears, I'll take your word for it."

"That's a good attitude," he said, then laughed as though he had a secret. "Try to hold on to it."

Maybe it did feel a little like Camelot, and maybe the crickets did sound like Merlin, Delilah thought with a smile. At least they might if she were the nice, pleasant woman she was pretending to be. If she were the kind of woman who believed in listening for magic.

And tonight I am, she told herself. *Tonight I'm exactly that kind of woman.*

Suddenly she threw her hands up in the air as she whirled around and shouted, "Hello!"

Bill laughed again, the sound coming from deep in his throat, and caught her waist with both hands. "Hello yourself, but you don't have to yell, I'm right here."

She loved the rich sound of his laughter. It made her feel even warmer than his smile did. "I wasn't helloing you," she said haughtily.

"Oh? Who were you helloing, Merlin?"

"Don't be silly, I never talk to crickets," she said regally. "That was simply my way of making my presence known. I was beginning to feel awed by everything—the night and the sand and the water and the sky." *And you,* she added silently. *Most of all you.* "That's not good. Awed is not good at all. I want to be a part of it, not a spectator."

He stared at her for a moment, smiling as though he found her and her silliness enchanting. Then he threw his head back and shouted, "Hello!"

She listened as his voice joined the wind, the water, the mariachi band, and the crickets. Then she laughed with pleasure. "You see? Now you're a part of it too."

"Now we're both a part of it," he agreed softly.

She closed her eyes and sighed. "Do you feel peculiar? All floaty, as though you were walking on the moon? I don't think it's the wine—that was excellent wine, by the way—because I had only two glasses."

"Three glasses."

She waved a dismissing hand. "Two glasses, three, it doesn't matter. Alcohol doesn't affect me. The group and I used to have parties that would last for days. I don't see how we all lasted through medical school. Booger and Jack can come up with some of the most lethal concoctions. There was one they called the Fuzzy Navel. It was—"

She broke off and looked up at him. "Whoops," she said quietly.

His lips curved in a slow smile as he moved a step closer. "Well, what do you know about that? Lovely Lila is a doctor. You know what this means, don't you?"

She backed away warily. "It means if you break your leg, medical attention is close at hand?"

He laughed and took another step toward her. "Not close enough." Catching her hand, he placed it firmly on his neck. "Not nearly close enough. It's time to pay the forfeit, lovely Lila."

She stared at him for a moment, then she shrugged and stood on tiptoes to press her lips to his. Delilah had intended the kiss to be a perfunctory one, a salute acknowledging the fact that he had won. That was what she had intended. She wasn't sure how the kiss went astray, but the minute her lips touched his, she knew it had.

She had never felt such compelling sweetness, had never expected to feel it. But there it was just the same. It swirled through her, pulling her closer to him, and even closer, because although she had never felt it she knew instantly that she wanted more.

Only a tiny part of the old hardhearted Delilah remained active, and that part nagged at her, demanding that she think logically.

It's the wine and the moonlight, the remnant of Delilah said. *It's being far away from the restrictions of home. It's because he's a stranger you'll never see again. That's the only reason it seems so special.*

But as he pulled her down to the sand with him, pressing his lean, hard body to hers, it felt like more. It felt like so much more.

Endless moments later, when she was drunk on the sweetness and wonder, he raised his head slightly to stare into her astounded eyes. "Lila," he whispered huskily.

"Yes?" Her voice was even more husky than his.

"That's all. Just Lila."

She drew in a deep breath. "We should probably . . . you know, start back or something."

"Or something," he agreed.

Although it was difficult to think with his body pressing into hers, the bit of hardhearted Delilah was growing stronger. "No, really," she said as firmly as she could. "We need to get back to the hotel."

He touched her face and said deliberately, "I'm a doctor too. Do you know what that means?"

"It means you can fix your own broken leg."

He chuckled. "It means that we have even more in common than we thought, but more important, it means that it is now my turn to pay the forfeit."

"No—"

But it was too late. He had already lowered his head, bringing his warm mouth to hers. And that was all it took for the incredible sweetness to begin again, as fresh and new and wonderful as the first time.

Life had rules. It had certainties. One certainty was that the woman who was Delilah Jones stood for reality. Delilah Jones was a hard-nosed, hard-hearted realist.

That had been a certainty yesterday. An hour earlier. Five minutes earlier. But it was no longer the case, for the realist seemed to have disappeared. In Bill's arms reality was suspended. There was no painful past. No uncertain future. Only this moment. This moment stretching into forever.

"Lila . . . Lila . . . Lila," he whispered against her throat.

"Yes . . . yes . . . yes," she whispered back, then they both laughed, at nothing, at everything.

He moved his fingers slowly up her throat, then cupped her face with both hands. They were strong hands, hands to depend on. And as he stared again into her eyes, Delilah saw a different world there, real but different from anything she had known. She felt herself being pulled into the world in his eyes. It was a place of warmth and happiness. A place where darkness wasn't allowed.

"Delilah?"

Although the word was spoken tentatively, it was nonetheless intrusive. Delilah reluctantly looked away from Bill and found Booger standing a foot away, shifting his feet as he looked down at them.

"Hello, Booger." Her voice was unrecognizably dreamy. "Isn't it a beautiful night?"

"I hate to bother you," Booger said hesitantly, "but Addie and I have joined forces, and we've got someone we want you to meet."

Bill didn't take his gaze from Delilah's face when he said, "He's too tall, Booger."

"Too tall?" Booger repeated in confusion.

"Or too round or too square. Too hot or too cold," Bill said, smiling down at Delilah. "He's the wrong one, Booger."

"Dee?" Booger said hesitantly.

"Listen to the man," Delilah said, returning Bill's smile. "He seems to know what he's talking about."

She didn't notice when Booger walked away because she had stepped again into the wonderful, secure world contained in Bill's eyes.

"I can't understand why you have that silly little piece of green in your eye," she murmured. "Is it there just to please me?"

"Why else would it be there? My mother says it's the devil in me trying to get out, but if it pleases you, then that's reason enough for it to be there."

"It pleases me."

"You please me," he whispered, his voice going hoarse again. "Everything about you pleases me because everything about you is special. If someone had asked me to dream the perfect woman, you would have been my dream."

She felt a hot wave of guilt wash over her, spoiling everything. The woman he was talking about, the special woman, wasn't Delilah. That woman didn't exist. She was a fabrication, a product of an imagination Delilah hadn't known she possessed until she had met Bill.

She couldn't let it continue. She had to stop it now, before it got too far out of hand. Bill was a wonderful man and shouldn't be made a fool of. Too wonderful.

"Bill, I'm not who you think I am," she whispered. "I'm not special. I—"

The rest of her confession was lost in his kiss. "Didn't anyone ever tell you not to contradict a man who's kissing your neck," he murmured as he moved his lips to her throat. When she shivered in sensual response he drew back a fraction of an inch to stare into her eyes. "I know what you are; I know who you are. You're the melody that's been playing across the back of my mind for years. Elusive, haunting, and so incredibly beautiful."

"I am?" she asked weakly.

"You are."

She wasn't, but, sweet heaven, she wished she were. At that moment she would have given anything to be the woman Bill thought she was.

What could it hurt to pretend for a while longer, she asked herself. The deed was already done; a few minutes more couldn't possibly make any difference. For just a little while she wanted to be someone special.

Raising one finger to outline his lips, she whispered, "Maybe you'd better kiss my neck again so I won't be able to contradict you."

Delilah wasn't sure how long her "little while" with Bill lasted. She knew only that the moon had moved quite a distance in the sky by the time they stood up and walked arm in arm back to the hotel.

Outside the door to her suite he leaned down and kissed her again, but this time it was as soft and light as an angel's kiss. Their eyes met for a moment, then she opened the door and went inside.

As soon as the door closed behind Delilah, Bill leaned against it and closed his eyes, a peculiar smile twisting his strong lips.

Lila.

Over and over again the name echoed through his mind, through his body, right to the center of him. There was no room for anything else because she filled him completely. Only Lila.

He was just an ordinary man. Why had he been chosen to receive such a gift? How could he have been so lucky? He had wanted to get away for a few days to take care of business and visit old friends. Then suddenly, without warning, heaven had dropped into his arms.

Bill didn't question the fact that he had fallen in love with her so quickly, so absolutely. He knew only that he had. But swiftly, he reminded himself to move slowly and carefully with her. She had loosened up a little tonight, but she was still a realist who didn't believe in Camelot or guardian angels. And she had been hurt badly. Life had taught her to be skeptical. It was going to be a tough job convincing her that magic had been at work tonight on the beach.

He laughed softly, remembering her wary reaction in the restaurant when he had told her he recognized her. He could imagine what she would say when he tried to convince her that they had found each other for a reason; that it wasn't merely a medical conference that had brought them both to Acapulco; that something fantastic had happened between them. She wouldn't believe him.

Walking toward the elevator, he whistled softly under his breath. She would be a tough nut to crack all right, but he had never looked forward to anything so much in his life. He would convince her. He had no doubt about it. One way or the other, he would.

Delilah leaned against the door in the darkened room. She couldn't seem to catch her breath. There was a sweet, warm fog in her brain, and it made everything feel out of kilter. The whole world had shifted sideways with the first touch of Bill's lips.

She couldn't understand it. Cool, calculating Delilah Jones was not supposed to feel this way. Never, never had she been carried away by emotions. Until now.

Was it possible that she had become so involved in the game of pretending to be a "normal" woman that she had begun to have the reactions a normal woman would have? That had to be it, she told herself firmly. She had simply been getting into her part. That was what made her feel so free, as though she hadn't a worry in the world.

Pushing away from the door, she frowned. Her life had never been without worries. There was always something dark lurking in the corners of her mind, memories from the past, fears for the future.

The fact that there was no darkness now made her positive that what she was feeling was not real. And Delilah needed reality. It was her only base. She wouldn't feel secure until she was her old pessimistic self again.

She shook her head. This conference was turning out to be more than she had bargained for. Everything had seemed so clear-cut, even this morning when she had walked off the plane. She remembered—it seemed ages ago instead of only hours—following her friends into the suite they had booked especially so they could all be together like in the old days. She had looked around at each of their faces, letting the feeling soak in.

As Delilah unpacked, lighthearted, nonsensical talk floated around the room. The scene was familiar and warm, bringing her a twinge of homesickness for the past.

So many times during their years of medical training the group had gathered exactly like this. That was back when they were all sharing a shabby old two-bedroom apartment, back before Glory married Alan, before they had all gone their separate ways to practice medicine.

Delilah looked back on those days as the most secure of her life. She hadn't been chosen a member of the group; she had more or less forced herself upon them. But they had accepted her. More than that, each in his own way had pulled her in and made her a part of his or her life.

She let her gaze linger on each of them in turn. Athos, Porthos, Aramis, D'Artagnan, and Moe.

That's what they had called themselves back then. They were an unlikely quintet, but somehow it worked, she thought, acknowledging their differences while giving thanks for the fate that had brought them all together back there in the beginning.

First there was Arnold Schlumburger, Booger to his friends. Even his name made her want to laugh. Booger, with his semi-psychotic sense of humor, was a genius. He was also the most loving person Delilah knew. He was a man who made secret sacrifices in order to boost the sagging ego of a friend in need. His brain and his humor had helped Delilah survive the ruthless years of medical training.

With his intelligence Booger could have gone into any field of medicine he chose, and he chose to practice family medicine as his father and grandfather had before him. Somehow, for Booger, it seemed right. After his residency in Dallas, Booger had gone home to Kansas to accept a partnership in his father's practice.

Next came Addie, a top-notch pediatrician. Addie was practical and prosaic and tough as an old boot on the outside. But on the inside she was as soft and vulnerable as a newborn kitten. Addie, the original California beach bunny, had surprised them all by joining Booger and Dr. Schlumburger in Kansas.

And then there was Jack. Mr. Moto seemed always to be preening. It was an integral part of his personality. The first things a stranger noticed about Jack were his straight black hair and the sexy eyes that were a gift of his Oriental heritage. But after a few minutes in his presence everything was overlooked in favor of his most outstanding characteristic: his giant ego. Jack was totally and happily self-absorbed—until one of his friends needed help. Then he became D'Artagnan and truly believed it was all for one and one for all. Jack was now a surgeon on staff at a prestigious Chicago hospital.

And last was Gloria Wainwright Spencer. Glory was more than Delilah's best friend. She was Delilah's heroine. Glory was what Delilah would give anything to be like. The younger woman had been loved and protected all her life, not only by her wealthy father, but by everyone who met her. However, that wasn't the part Delilah envied—at least not much. What Delilah envied most about Glory was her strength of character. She hadn't allowed her pampered background to weaken her. She fought for what she knew was right. Glory had great integrity and refused to compromise it. Glory and Delilah were internists and had both stayed in Dallas to practice medicine, Glory at a teaching hospital, Delilah in private practice.

Delilah cared very much for each member of the group, but she would never tell them so. And she wouldn't let them know how desperately she had missed them in the years they had been apart. She had built an image for herself that didn't allow for sentimentality. The group expected her to be sophisticated, reserved, and fearless, and Delilah saw no reason to change that.

"Okay," Jack said, grabbing Delilah's arm to pull her down to the bed. "Tell me why some man hasn't lassoed you by now."

Delilah smiled carefully. "It's not all that difficult to understand," she said, keeping her voice casual. "I happen to have exacting standards, uncompromising standards. I want a man who is intelligent, personable, and who happens to be very, *very* wealthy. Is that too much to ask?"

They all laughed just as she had intended them to. "I told you all a long time ago that I became a doctor only so I could make lots of money," she said matter-of-factly, "and because as a doctor I would be thrown into the company of wealthy men, which meant I would stand a good chance of marrying a man who also makes a lot of money."

Glory gave an inelegant snort. "Yes, that's what you told us, and that may be why you got into medicine initially, but it's not why you stayed with it. I've seen you with patients, remember? I would give my eye teeth to be even half as good a diagnostician as you are."

Delilah ignored her. "I've managed to stake a claim for myself in Dallas, but you all know what it's like for new doctors. Does anyone want to talk about the cost of malpractice insurance?" For a second every face looked grim. "A doctor's income simply isn't as secure as it used to be. Which is why I'm looking for someone who has a healthy practice already established. And to be perfectly frank, I can't afford to waste any more time."

As Delilah glanced around at her friends, she

realized they couldn't possibly understand what was driving her. They were too secure, too normal to comprehend the desperation behind her decision. They couldn't know that the reason she so much envied Glory's integrity was that Delilah couldn't afford that particular luxury.

"It was when I saw that a nonmedical man wouldn't work that I changed my mind about coming to the conference several days early like the rest of you. It's time for me to get serious."

She paused, letting her gaze pass over each of them in turn, letting the suspense build until they were all looking at her expectantly.

"At this conference I'm hunting," she said slowly, then smiled. "At this conference, my friends, I'm going to bag me a man."

The silence in the room became electrified, and looking at her friends' stunned faces, Delilah had trouble maintaining her usual Madonna smile.

After a few moments Booger cleared his throat noisily and rose to his feet. "For a friend, I'm prepared to make the ultimate sacrifice." He took Delilah's hand, then dropped to one knee. "Marry me, Delilah. Come with me to Kansas. Be the mother of my warped little children—twelve or thirteen would be nice. I'm not rich yet, but I'm my father's only heir. Dad will love you . . . we can swear he's senile, stick him in a nursing home, and—"

"Booger!"

"Okay, okay. We'll kill him. Then we can live the good life until they catch us. What do you say?"

Arching one brow, Delilah stared down at him for a long moment. "It sounds interesting, not to mention macabre, but in a word, no."

"Okay," he said agreeably. "On to Plan Two. Someone help me up." When he was on his feet again, he glanced around at the others. "I propose—"

Addie snorted loudly. "You propose too damn much. You propose to waitresses who refill your coffee cup and to women who buy chocolate-covered doughnuts and to anyone, no matter what their gender, who is wearing jogging shorts."

"As I was saying," Booger continued, pointedly ignoring the interruption, "I propose that we help Dee find a husband by having a scavenger hunt."

Now, as she heard the echoes of that conversation, Delilah was doubly glad she hadn't let Bill know what she and her friends were involved in, hadn't let him know that she was on a cold-blooded husband-hunt. She didn't want Bill in her life, not her real life. It wasn't the place for a man like him.

She had made her plan and she would stick to it, come hell or high water. She would marry a man who could give her the security she so desperately craved; a man who wanted an intelligent, personable wife; a man who didn't expect or want the impossible from her; a man who didn't need her love. Because that was something she would never give away again.

Straightening her back in determination, she walked into the bedroom she was sharing with

Addie and stood for a moment to allow her eyes to adjust to the darkness.

"Delilah?" The light between the beds snapped on. Addie, squinting from the bright light and looking vulnerable without her thick glasses, moved her head, trying to locate her roommate. "I wondered if you were coming back tonight," she said to the cheval mirror.

"I guess I lost track of time. Is it late?" Delilah glanced at her watch and whistled in surprise. It was after three. "Where did the night go?"

Addie, guided by Delilah's voice, was now able to locate her general position. "Yeah, where?" she grumbled. "We expected to see you at dinner."

"Bill took me to a little restaurant down the beach. Then, as you know, we stayed on the beach . . . talking. I hope no one missed me."

"Booger did." Addie sat up and wrapped her arms around her knees. Her sleeping attire consisted solely of a T-shirt with I DON'T DO MORNINGS printed on the front. "That's why he insisted on tracking you down so you could check out the man we found."

Delilah paused in taking off her clothes and glanced up. There was a strange tone in Addie's voice. "What's up?"

Addie leaned back against the padded headboard. "Dee, I need to talk to you."

Delilah took off her skirt and walked to the closet. "So talk."

"It's just—" Addie broke off and hit the mattress with both fists. "Dammit, you have men falling all over you . . . like that adorable Bill you were with tonight. You don't have to do anything, you don't even have to say a word. You simply walk into a room and they all start drooling. How can I do that? Short of plastic surgery, I mean."

"Don't be silly. You're very attractive."

Addie grimaced. "You're a friend. You have to say things like that."

"Bill said you were adorable, remember?"

Addie smiled. "He did, didn't he? But Bill's different. I think he would make any woman feel attractive."

Delilah frowned. Maybe Addie was right. Maybe she had run into one of those men who had a natural talent for making any woman he came in contact with feel special, feel as though she were the only woman in the world. That would explain what Delilah had felt tonight. What she still felt, she corrected herself silently.

Glancing up, she cleared her throat. There was no need to tell Addie her conclusions. "Bill wasn't pretending. He really thought you were cute. Everyone does."

"*Cute*," Addie repeated in disgust. "Cartoons are cute. Dogs are cute. Even some bugs are cute. I don't want to be cute. I want to be sexy as all get-out. I want men to *lust* after me, Dee."

"Cute was obviously a poor choice of words," Delilah said dryly.

"How about sexy?"

"Sexy is a subjective thing, Addie. I'm not qualified to judge that. Attractive certainly. Everyone thinks you're attractive."

"Not Booger."

Delilah was stunned. All the yearning in the world seemed to be in those two words. She didn't know whether to laugh or cry. "You're in love with *Booger*?"

"I thought you knew. Glory does."

"Glory is extremely perceptive, especially when it comes to affairs of the heart. I think that was left out of my original equipment," Delilah added with a shrug.

"I've been in love with him *forever*. Why do you think I gave up California? I mean, do I really look like a Kansas sort of person? People wear socks in Kansas. I traded beaches and 'anything goes' for tornadoes and 'quaint.' I don't fit in, but I can fake it if it means being with Booger. I had to do some really wild manipulating to persuade Dr. Schlumburger to take me into his practice along with his son."

"Hasn't working together brought you closer?"

"Sure." Addie's voice was heavy with dejection. "We're as close as any two buddies can be. He simply refuses to see me as a woman." Her lips trembled as she met Delilah's gaze. "What am I going to do, Dee?"

Delilah glanced away from the desperation in Addie's myopic eyes. "This is Glory's territory, not mine," she said gruffly. "She's the one who gives aid and comfort to people with problems."

"I can't talk to Glory. She's distracted and moody. I can't hit her with my trouble if she has trouble of her own."

Delilah was instantly alert. Had Glory been different lately, she wondered.

Almost four years ago, when Glory first met her husband, Delilah had seen then how much her friend loved Alan. Only a blind fool could have missed it. The evidence was in Glory's face, in her every look. And from the beginning Delilah had been afraid for her friend. It was risky to love at all, but it was insane and self-destructive to love that much.

Although both she and Glory lived in Dallas, Delilah didn't see Glory often. Being around a couple so obviously devoted to each other made Delilah more than a little uncomfortable. It wasn't that they made her feel like a fifth wheel; the problem was that Delilah knew love for what it was. She had always known. Love was a chain-wrapped specter from her past. It was her own private hell.

For most of the people Delilah had known, love was a meshing of weaknesses, a do-it-yourself kit with no instructions included. If you asked ten people to define love, you would get ten different answers. But no matter what definition they put on it, there was always a qualifying statement added—sooner or later, love hurts.

That was the truth as Delilah knew it, but when she saw Glory and Alan together the truth sometimes became confused. If they were right, then Delilah had to be wrong. And if Delilah were wrong about love, her entire life had been built on that error.

No, she told herself, she wasn't wrong. She couldn't be. Glory and Alan were the exception that proved the rule. They were unique.

Delilah would never allow herself to depend on another human being for happiness the way Glory did. That was the way to suicide row.

"Couldn't you give me a few tips?"

Addie's voice pulled Delilah abruptly out of her dark introspection.

"Please, Delilah, I'm really desperate," Addie begged.

Delilah did not want to do this. She felt extremely uncomfortable with the idea of being an emotional—or sexual—counselor to anyone. For heaven's sake, she was the last person in the world to give advice on love.

"I don't know what to tell you, Addie," she said, her voice hesitant. "This really isn't my kind of—"

Delilah broke off when she saw the sheen of tears in her friend's eyes. "Oh, hell," she said in exasperation. "All right . . . all right. I'll try to think of something. But don't blame me if it's all wrong."

Addie scrambled to her knees, her expression brightening. "I knew you'd come through for me. Thank you, Dee. Thank you, thank you, thank—"

"If you hug me, you can forget the whole thing," Delilah said, watching her warily.

Addie shook her head vehemently. "No, I won't. I promise."

Delilah sat on the bed beside her friend and stared into space as she considered what Addie had told her. After a moment she said, "Why don't you simply tell him how you feel? I admit I don't usually advocate honesty between the sexes, but in your case, it seems to fit."

Addie shook her head. "I couldn't do that. If I can't have his love, I want at least to keep his friendship. If I tell Booger I love him, he might feel uncomfortable around me. Or pity me." She shuddered violently. "I don't think I could stand that."

Delilah understood. She had never been able to handle pity either. "Okay, I'll think of something else." She paused and chewed thoughtfully on her lip. "Maybe you should make use of this buddy thing."

"What do you mean?"

"I haven't got it all worked out yet, but the first thing you're going to do is buy some new clothes. Trash all your Valley Girl stuff and buy things that are feminine. Not frilly, you're not a frilly sort of person. Look for things that are subtly seductive. If you don't know what you're looking for, ask a salesclerk who looks sexy herself."

"I couldn't do that," Addie said, her voice shocked. "Booger would notice immediately. He'd make fun of me."

"We want him to notice," Delilah said. "And if he makes jokes, you simply laugh and throw in jokes of your own. Then tell him an edited version of the truth. Tell him that you've decided I have the right idea about finding a husband at this conference. Tell him you're in your sexual prime. You want babies and a home life. Throw in all the stuff about your biological clock."

Addie frowned. "What good will all that do?"

"Booger's sharp, Addie." Delilah smiled confidently. "He's going to start giving some thought to what it will be like when the attention you usually give to him goes to your husband instead. That's enough for the first step."

For a long time Addie sat staring at the ceiling. She didn't say anything, but several times she nodded, as though she were holding a silent dialogue with herself, and Delilah could almost see the gears in her friend's brain clicking.

Later, when the room was dark and Delilah lay in bed, it suddenly hit her that she, Delilah Jones, the woman who never meddled in other people's affairs, had done just exactly that. Big time, she thought wryly.

Without warning, another piece of her world had shifted beneath her feet.

Five

"I wish you'd hurry up and choose someone, Dee," Jack grumbled. "I've approached so many men, people are beginning to look at me funny."

Jack, Booger, Glory, Alan, and Delilah were having breakfast on the terrace of the hotel. For the last ten minutes they had all been discussing the hazards involved in finding Delilah a husband. Delilah knew she should be paying closer attention —it was her future, after all—but she couldn't seem to work up any interest.

It was Bill's fault, she thought grumpily. He of the lost-puppy cuteness and patchwork-quilt eyes.

She had told herself everything would be back to normal this morning. She had told herself that passing fancy was a concept she had finally discovered. She had told herself a lot of things, but the fact was that every time she thought of Bill— which was much too often for comfort—the floaty, moonwalking sensation returned.

It was no wonder Delilah was now in an extremely irritable mood.

The night before, she hadn't been able to take in the fact that Bill was a doctor. But it was the first thought that had come to her when she had opened her eyes in the morning. And the thought had been tinged with a moment of deep regret that had surprised her.

Bill was a doctor. She was looking for a doctor. But Bill wasn't the kind of doctor she needed. He didn't have the attitude or wardrobe that were the unmistakable signatures of a successful doctor.

When Delilah first decided to study medicine, she had assumed that all doctors were extremely wealthy. It hadn't taken her long to realize how wrong she had been. The truly successful doctors were the ones who specialized and cultivated important patients. They worked to build a name in the world as well as in the medical community. They considered medicine a business just like any other business.

And that was the kind of doctor Delilah had to find.

Until a few years before she had fallen in with the group, Delilah had spent most of her time fighting to survive, wondering where her next meal was coming from, wondering if she would have a place to sleep for the night. She had been fighting and wondering and worrying since she was fourteen years old. She knew only too well what life could be like without money, and she wouldn't be secure until there was no possibility of that happening again.

Why did she have to keep telling herself that, she wondered, frowning fiercely. Why did she have to keep reminding herself that Bill was completely wrong for her?

Bill was nothing to her. She would put him out of her mind. Right now. She wouldn't think about the way his hair fell across his forehead. She wouldn't think about his absurdly appealing smile. She wouldn't wonder how long he was going to stay in the village of Nuevo Oviedo with his friends.

She wouldn't, she told herself, then turned her attention back to her own friends.

"You're going about the scavenger hunt all wrong, Jack," Booger was saying as he wiped jelly from his chin. "You should have worked out a plan, like I did."

"What plan?" Jack asked with open skepticism.

"I tell the men I approach that I'm working on a survey for the AMA. Then I can ask them anything I want from income after taxes to the size of their . . . well, shoes."

Glory laughed. "Shoe size is the first thing I check too," she said, her eyes sparkling. "I don't have a plan, but no one seems to mind giving me information."

"And that's what bothers me," Alan said ruefully. "You've got men following you everywhere. I think from now on I'd better go with you on this manhunt."

Smiling at his attitude of mock jealousy, Delilah

took a moment to study Alan. He was dark—dark hair, dark skin—and the scar on his cheek made him seem rather fierce at times. But when he looked at Glory there was no fierceness. He always looked at his wife as though she were life itself.

Switching her gaze to Glory, Delilah searched for signs of moodiness. After a moment she gave it up. Glory looked as contented as she had every right to be. Delilah could see no hint of the turmoil Addie had mentioned.

Glancing around the table, Delilah said, "Where is Addie? She was up disgustingly early."

"Here I am."

They turned as one, and all did a double take when they saw Addie. She had blossomed. Her hair, instead of being drawn back in a French braid, curled wildly around her face. She wore shorts, as usual, but the colors and fabric were softer and more feminine. The biggest change was in her face. Addie no longer wore the enormous, thick-lensed glasses, which was probably why, at that moment, she ran into a table and knocked over several glasses of water.

Booger stood up and went to her. "Jeez, Addie, where are your glasses?"

"I stepped on them," she said breathlessly as she clutched Booger's arm. "I couldn't see to find them because I wasn't wearing them so I stepped on them. I guess I'll have to feel my way around for the next few days."

"You're kidding," he said, leading her to the

table. "We're supposed to go sight-seeing today. What are you gonna do, go sight-*feeling*?"

"You'll have to lead me, Boog. I trust you . . . but keep us away from the cliffs."

"Where are we going today anyway?" Jack asked the group at large. "'I'm fed up with husband hunting. And I'd like to see something besides hotel lobbies."

When a debate began on where to spend the day, Delilah tried to listen. She even tried to contribute to the conversation. But a little voice in the back of her head kept saying, "Don't think of Bill. Don't think of Bill."

"Dammit, I'm not!" she said in exasperation. When everyone at the table turned to stare at her, Delilah coughed and added, "I'm not . . . um . . . really in the mood to go deep-sea fishing."

"We wouldn't force you to do anything you dislike so vehemently," Jack said warily. "Why don't you make a suggestion?"

Delilah glanced down at her plate. "When I travel, I always like to get away from the tourist areas and see how the people really live."

"Yeah, I like that too."

"Sounds great to me."

"Then it's decided," Alan said. "I'll ask the concierge to give us a list of places that aren't too far away."

"That won't be necessary." Delilah lifted her gaze to the mountains, her lips curving in a self-mocking smile. "I know a place that's just exactly what we're looking for."

• • •

Bill stood on the north side of Nuevo Oviedo's central plaza, smiling with pleasure as he gazed around. On one side of the plaza was a simple but beautiful old stone church, the heart of the community. The remaining three sides were lined with stores and government buildings. In the center of the square a small fountain sparkled in the sunlight. It was surrounded by stone benches and a lushly flowering garden.

Bill had come to Nuevo Oviedo to see Arturo Fuentes, the village doctor. He had met Arturo several years before in Houston and had become intrigued by the village even before setting eyes on it. Now he considered it his special place. He had made good, solid friends here.

He wanted to share all the beauty and the friends with Lila. He wanted it to be special for her too.

Life was so funny, he thought with a smile. He hadn't realized until he saw her that he had been looking for her. He hadn't known that he was loose pieces of a jigsaw puzzle. One look at Lila and the pieces came together. Now his life made sense.

Damn, he felt good. He wanted to grab the people walking by and say, *Let me tell you about Lila. Let me tell you about the most wonderful woman in the world.*

But he didn't. He simply walked along, hands in pockets, whistling softly under his breath. It was a beautiful day. An almost perfect day.

Seconds later Bill glanced up, and suddenly the almost perfect day became absolutely perfect.

Delilah sat on a stone bench watching the water in a small fountain dance in the sunlight. She had told the others that she preferred to explore alone and that she would meet them in three hours.

Lies. All lies. She didn't want to be alone. She wanted to be with Bill.

She had made no attempt at self-deception about her reasons for coming to Nuevo Oviedo. She had wanted one more taste of the other side of life. The sweet side. The side where maneuvering and manipulating were foreign things.

Suddenly she heard him call her name, and, smiling, she glanced up to see him walking toward her. When she recognized the undisguised look of joy on Bill's face, her smile faded slightly as she felt a sudden unexpected need to protect him. From herself.

He was so damned open. One had a duty, whether one liked it or not, to protect people who made themselves this vulnerable. Bill was a sweet man, and she was deceiving him by pretending to be something she wasn't.

She would stop it soon, she promised herself. She would make sure he wasn't hurt by her pretense. She would be with him for just one more day, then she would end the charade.

"How can you look so glamorous and still look

like you belong here?" he asked as he reached her.

"Walking shorts and a madras shirt do not glamour make," she said, then studied his face. "You don't seem surprised to see me."

His hand dropped to her waist, and he gave it a squeeze as he shook his head. "Surprised? No, I guess not. You see, you were with me already." When she raised a questioning brow, he laughed. "I was thinking of you, and suddenly you were here. I invoked you."

"I don't know whether to be flattered or offended," she said with a laugh. "*Invoke* sounds like something you would do with a curse."

"Or an enchantment," he said softly, keeping his gaze on her face. "How long do I have you? Do you have time for lunch with some friends of mine?"

"I have time, but surely they won't want a stranger dropping in on them out of the blue."

He smiled down at her. "They'll fall in love with you. How could they not?"

And how could she not feel a burst of warmth when he looked at her with such open pleasure? Rising to her feet, she let him take her arm and guide her.

The large, low house, built of wood rather than adobe because of the frequent rain, sat on the edge of the village. The beautiful flowering bushes that surrounded the house disguised the fact that it wasn't a wealthy household.

The front door was opened for them by a woman

in a pink housedress. Although the woman seemed as though she were normally shy, her excitement on seeing Bill was open and exuberant. She threw her arms around him and spoke rapidly in Spanish.

Laughing, Bill pulled Delilah forward. "Lila, I'd like you to meet the best dancer in all of Mexico, Alicia Fuentes."

As they spoke, a group of children had crowded into the area immediately behind Alicia. She shooed the children away just as Bill began putting names to the faces. Along with the expected Juans and Marias there were several names Delilah had never heard and feared she wouldn't be able to remember.

Inside the house there were more introductions as Delilah was presented to the fathers, mothers, older brothers, and sisters of the children who had been at the door. Other than Alicia, only two or three of the Fuentes group spoke English, but all of them, without exception, made her welcome.

Bill gripped Delilah's arm and smiled an enigmatic, slightly wicked smile. "Now it's time for you to meet *Abuelo*."

"*Sí, sí, Abuelo*," several of the adults murmured, heads nodding, eyes sparkling.

Bill moved her through the group to where an old man was seated against the wall in a high-back carved wooden chair that reminded Delilah of a throne. He had iron-gray hair and his dark face was as intricately carved as the chair.

Bill spoke to him rapidly in Spanish and, it seemed to Delilah, at great length. Finally he turned to Delilah and said, "Lila, this is Tomás Fuentes, *Abuelo*, Grandfather, to most of the people in this house."

The old man didn't move. He simply stared at her for a long time. After a few moments Delilah began to grow uncomfortable, but she refused to look away from his dark eyes. Behind her, the people in the room seemed to be holding their collective breath.

Then suddenly Señor Fuentes nodded his head abruptly and said, *"Bueno, Guillermo, bueno."*

Immediately everyone relaxed and began talking and laughing. Delilah felt she had just passed some kind of test and didn't know whether to be annoyed or amused.

Before she could decide, the Fuentes clan began to move en masse into the dining room. It was a large, high-ceilinged room that was almost completely filled by a long wooden table. A high-back chair stood at each end of the table, and there were benches on either side.

Alicia indicated that Delilah was to sit at the end of the table, opposite Señor Fuentes, but she hesitated. "Shouldn't Bill sit there?" she asked. "He's your special guest. I'm just a tag-along."

"No, no, you sit here," Alicia said, giving her a shy smile. "You are our honored guest. Guillermo is family, as you will be soon."

Delilah turned to Bill, who was seated on her right, and whispered, "If they insist on adopting everyone who walks in off the street, it's no wonder they have such a large family."

He laughed, but there was a peculiar look in his eyes, a pleased look that made her wonder what was going on. He had been very casual about the invitation, maybe too casual. Why should this family accept her so completely?

Delilah was used to struggling for acceptance, and life had taught her to be suspicious of good things that came easily. There was always a price to pay.

Later, she told herself, she would figure the whole thing out. She was an expert at finding angles. This situation would prove no exception.

Lunch turned out to be an informal affair with lots of food, talk, and laughter. Everyone at the table seemed to be trying to fatten up Delilah. First one then another of the Fuentes family would bring a side dish or an alternate entree for her inspection and, supposedly, her consumption. Delilah didn't want to hurt anyone's feelings, but even Booger couldn't have done justice to the tremendous meal.

After lunch everyone except the women and children who were in charge of cleaning up went outside to the patio. The children immediately surrounded Delilah, taking her on a tour of the yard as they and some of the younger women tried to teach her some Spanish words.

Jaime, a precociously flirtatious seven-year-old, stooped to pick up a handful of soil. "*Tierra*," he said carefully.

She pointed to his face, the face that had been

spotless minutes earlier. *"Tierra,"* she repeated to the noisy amusement of the others.

On the other side of the patio Bill sat with the men of the Fuentes family who were all clustered around old Señor Fuentes. The expressions on their faces were uniformly serious, and several times one or the other of the men would get loud and vehement. The old man would simply raise his eyes to the offender, who would immediately back down.

Delilah recalled what Bill had told her about the way Tomás Fuentes ran the village. She still believed he was a tyrannical old man, but she could see now that he didn't take his responsibilities lightly.

Little more than an hour later, when she and Bill left the Fuentes house, the children walked along with them to the marketplace. There were rows of wooden stalls and wares displayed on blankets spread on the ground. Fruit, vegetables, chickens, and trinkets filled the area. But there were no people.

"Siesta time," Bill said apologetically when Delilah found a red leather belt that made her eyes light up. "We'll have to come back for it later."

Before long they were on the opposite side of the village from the Fuentes house. One by one the children stepped forward and spoke to Delilah in polite but incomprehensible words. When the last one finished, Delilah smiled and thanked them as well as she could in her meager Spanish.

As soon as the children had scattered, Bill took

her hand and pulled her into the thick forest that grew right to the edge of the village.

"Where are we going?" she asked as the thick growth closed behind them, obscuring all sight of the village.

"I want to show you something." He glanced back at her. "How did you like my friends?"

"They were wonderful," she said with enthusiasm. "And I loved the family feel of the place. You could tell the children are very much loved there." She paused. "And as much as I hate to admit it, I even liked Señor Fuentes. He's a formidable old man, but there's a kind of old world, autocratic charm about him. He must have knocked the women dead with those dark eyes when he was younger. How old is he anyway?"

"No one knows. And no one has nerve enough to ask. We do know he was born before births were regularly recorded here." He held a tree limb aside for her. "*Abuelo* has lived his whole life in Nuevo Oviedo. It's his village and he wants things for it. He has dreams for it."

"Prosperity?"

He shook his head. "No, like you, he's a realist. He knows Nuevo Oviedo will never be a wealthy village, but he wants things for the village that would normally come only with wealth. He wants quality education for the children and a chance for them to go to college. He wants co-op farming and improved techniques. He wants a local hospital. He spends all his time and energy making plans and talking to influential people." Bill laughed. "I think it's just plain stubbornness that keeps him alive. He won't let go until he's sure his plans are under way."

The old man was certainly impressive, Delilah admitted silently. That much responsibility would tend to make anyone autocratic. "Does he have a heart condition?"

"What makes you ask that?"

"My high school Spanish wasn't much help, but when you were introducing me to him, I thought I recognized a couple of words. One was *corazón*. Doesn't that mean heart? I assumed there must be something wrong with his heart."

"Not his. Mine." He raised his gaze to her face. "*Mi corazón*," he said softly.

Delilah couldn't look away from his eyes. So much gentle warmth. So much caring. And for the first time in her life, Delilah Jones blushed.

She tried to pull herself back to earth by reminding herself that Spanish was an ornate language, an extravagant language. People probably used *mi corazón* when introducing their dentists. But it didn't do any good. She stared into his eyes and went back to the safe, warm place she had found last night. She had missed it.

After a long moment he glanced over her shoulder and said, "Look, Lila."

She turned slowly, then stopped as her breath caught in her throat.

They stood on a cliff that looked out over a deep green gorge. At the north end a slender thread of a waterfall fell hundreds of feet to the floor of the valley, filling it with a fine silver mist. And everywhere she looked there were rainbows.

"You brought me here to share heaven with me," she whispered in awe.

"No, that's not heaven," he said, turning her to press her against a tree. "This is heaven."

When he wrapped his arms around her and brought his mouth to hers, she knew this was what she had been waiting for. This was what she had been aching for since he had left her at the door in the small hours of the morning.

She willed her mind to go blank. She didn't want to think; she wanted only to feel. And as his hard, exciting body began to move urgently against hers, she did just exactly that. She gave herself over completely to sensation, sweet sensation.

For a long time she forgot where they were. She forgot who they were. She simply reveled in the feel of his lips on hers, his body against hers.

"Have dinner with me tonight." His voice was rough and breathless as though he had just run a long way.

She dropped her head against his chest, feeling weak. "I can't." The words were almost a groan. "I've already made plans to go out with my friends."

"They're important to you." He sounded as though he wasn't quite sure he liked the idea.

"Yes, they're important. For years we took care of one another. And this is the first time we've all been together in over three years."

She didn't know why it was so important that he understand. She had always made it a rule never to explain or make excuses for her actions. But with Bill it was different. She cared what he thought about her. She cared.

He kissed her again, holding her even tighter. "Just a drink then. After dinner meet me in the bar at La Porta for a drink."

"Just a drink?" she asked, feeling her resolve weaken.

He touched her face gently and sighed. "No, that was a lie. It won't be just a drink. We both want more than that."

He moved his lower body against hers, igniting fires. "Feel what happens to us when we come together," he whispered huskily. "We've known each other for only two days, but that doesn't matter. It feels like coming home. It feels like returning to a place that's familiar but more wonderful than you ever dreamed it could be. There's a rightness when we touch . . . you've got to feel it too. You must."

She felt it all right. She felt too much, and it confused her. Delilah couldn't understand what was happening to her. She had always used men's desire for her as a tool. She gave enough only to accomplish her goals, and she always knew when to back off. But she couldn't tell Bill that.

Suddenly it was very important that for the little time they had left together he think well of her. She wouldn't meet him for a drink. She wouldn't see him again at all. She would leave him thinking she was a nice, ordinary woman.

It was best for him. Best for her too. When she was with him her objective views of life began to slide away, and that couldn't happen.

Drawing upon all her strength, she said, "I'm sorry, Bill. I won't be able to meet you for a drink or anything else. I have prior commitments."

For a moment he showed no reaction. Then when he suddenly relaxed, Delilah realized how stiffly he had been holding himself.

He smiled down at her. "I'll be in the bar at ten, just in case," he said quietly.

"But—"

"I'll be waiting, Lila."

Six

"Are you sure I look all right?" Addie asked anxiously as she and Delilah crossed the small lobby of the hotel. They were on their way to join the rest of the group for dinner at the Wimberley.

"For Pete's sake, Addie, I've told you at least thirty times that you look gorgeous."

Delilah was telling her nervous friend nothing less than the truth. The simple but form-fitting dress and dramatic evening makeup gave Addie a completely different look. Instead of looking like the slightly wacky girl next door, she now looked like a provocative elf.

Grabbing Delilah's arm, Addie pulled her abruptly to a halt. "Wait!" Her unfocused eyes were wide with panic. "My mind has gone blank. After dinner I'm supposed to tell Booger that I need to walk on the beach to clear my head and that he has to come to keep me from walking into the ocean." She swallowed hard. "I forget the rest! This isn't going to work. I'll only end up making a fool of myself."

She swung around frantically and began to walk in the opposite direction. "I'm going back to the suite to hide under the bed," Addie called back over her shoulder. "Tell them that I broke a leg. Tell them I've been hijacked to Cuba."

Laughing helplessly, Delilah caught up with Addie and put both hands on her friend's shoulders to turn her around and push her toward the Wimberley. "You're an idiot."

"And that's another reason I should go back to the room," Addie said. "Why didn't I wear a dress like yours? Why didn't I get something with a high neck? Why didn't I become a nun like Janet Marie Henderson?" She gulped in air, then moaned. "I'm scared, Dee. I'm really, really scared. It was much easier dreaming about Booger."

"Dreams don't make babies," Delilah said flatly. "Just relax. Nothing is going to go wrong. You're supposed to tell him how inadequate you feel as a husband hunter—which is nothing but the truth. Then you suddenly notice that he's a man. You ask him what a man likes in the way of a kiss. Aggressive? Demure? He tells you what he likes, but you're a little slow and don't quite understand, so you ask him to demonstrate. That's it. Corny but effective. And simple as pie."

"I think I'm going to be sick."

"Addie," Delilah said sternly, "I forbid you to be sick. Come on, we're almost there. Do exactly what I told you, and I promise everything will work out fine."

When the two women walked into the restaurant just off the lobby of the Wimberley, heads turned. Delilah was used to it and didn't notice until Addie began pulling at the low neckline of her dress.

"Stop that," Delilah said. "They're not staring because there's something wrong with you. They're staring because two beautiful women just walked into the room."

"Two?" Addie said doubtfully.

"Just wait and see," Delilah said confidently.

As they drew near the table, Alan stood up and Delilah could have kissed him when he whistled, muttering, "Va-va-va-*voom*," as he pulled Addie's chair out for her.

The noises that Jack made were disgusting but just as effective. "I've always thought there should be some kind of law that forces women to show a certain amount of cleavage," he said, then glanced at the high neckline of Delilah's deep purple dress. "You'd be under arrest, Dee."

"One of these days someone is going to clear the trash out of your brain," Delilah said with a sweet smile, "and there won't be anything left."

As she squabbled with Jack, Delilah kept an eye on Booger. He couldn't stop staring at Addie. He didn't say anything. He simply sat, looking confused and more than a little intrigued.

Smiling in satisfaction, Delilah straightened in her chair and suddenly noticed there was a stranger sitting across the table from her. A man.

Jack, a suspicious twinkle in his eye, said,

"Delilah, I'd like you to meet Dr. Stephen French. He's a urologist. Steve, this is our delectable Delilah, Dr. Delilah Jones. She's in internal medicine."

If Jack had been close enough, Delilah would have kicked him in the shin. Knowing him, he had probably chosen a seat well away from her for that very reason.

After their drinks were served, Steve leaned across the table toward her. "Would you like to dance, Delilah?"

"Thank you," she murmured, "I'd love to."

Why did I say that, she wondered as she pushed back her chair. She didn't want to dance. Even if she had wanted to dance, there was only one man she wanted to dance with. And he wasn't there.

"So you're an internist," Steve said as soon as they were on the dance floor.

"Yes. And you're a urologist."

She raised her wrist slightly from where it lay on his shoulder. Eight-thirty. Only an hour and a half until Bill would be in the bar.

"You practice in Dallas?"

"Yes, and you?"

"Milwaukee."

Bill wouldn't be there, she told herself. Men had so many handy little lines they threw at women. *I'll be waiting, Lila.* That was right up there with "My wife doesn't understand me" and "I've had a vasectomy."

Even if he did show up at the bar, it was nothing to her. She was having a fine time without him.

"I hear the weather's always good in Dallas."

"Usually," she said, glancing again at her watch. "Do you get much rain in Milwaukee?"

"About average, I guess."

A fine time, she repeated silently, gritting her teeth.

Bill was probably eating dinner now. Alone? She shook her head slightly in irritation. It didn't matter if he was alone or not. It didn't matter if he was smiling at someone else, showing his crooked front teeth. It didn't matter if he was putting on his puppy-dog act for another woman. It *really* didn't matter.

Steve was in the middle of telling her about the women in his life—his ex-wife, his ex-girlfriend—and Delilah was in the middle of remembering how Bill's lips felt on hers when she finally decided she had better start paying attention to her dance partner.

She tried. She really, honestly tried. But as Delilah watched Steve's face, she became mesmerized by a mole that moved up and down while he talked.

This is the man Jack brought. This is the mole that sits on the cheek of the man Jack brought. This is the hair that grows from the mole that sits on the cheek of the man Jack brought.

Stop that! she told herself, swallowing a giggle. In spite of the mole, Steve was an attractive man. An interesting man. A successful, wealthy man. He was exactly what the doctor ordered.

Play the Loveswept Match Game

AND GET AS MANY AS SEVEN FREE

THERE'S NO COST! NO OBLIGATIO
AND NO PURCHASE NECESSAR

HOW TO PLAY:

1. Carefully scratch off the three boxes at t
and match one, two, or three hearts wit
hearts already revealed. You are eligible
one or more free books, and possibly ot
depending on how many hearts you m

2. When you return the postage-paid card
send you the books and gifts you quali
absolutely free.

3. A month later, we'll send you 6 new L
novels to preview. You always get 15 d
preview them, before you decide. If y
to keep them, each book is yours for o
— a savings of 41¢ per book (plus post
handling).

4. You'll always receive your Loveswept
before they are available in stores. Yo
first to thrill to these exciting new st

FREE—LIGHTED MAKEUP CASE

You may qualify to receive this tortoise-shell makeup case—if you match three hearts.

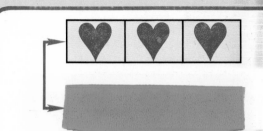
(DETACH AND MAIL CARD TODAY)

NO RISK GUARANTEE:

There's no obligation to buy — the free gifts are mine to keep. I may preview each shipment for 15 days. If I don't want it, I simply return the books within 15 days and owe nothing. If I keep them I will pay just $12.50 (I save $2.50 off the retail price for 6 books) plus postage and handling.

(DETACH AND MAIL CARD TODAY)

And Delilah couldn't have been more miserable. No matter how attractive and successful and interesting he was, he wasn't Bill.

All through dinner she found herself glancing at her watch. By ten-thirty she was a mental case. She tried desperately to keep her mind on what Steve and her friends were saying, but her thoughts kept going back to Bill. Every time someone laughed, she remembered Bill's laugh. When the waiter brought their dessert, she thought of dessert at the Fuentes house with Bill beside her.

And every time she thought of him she withdrew a little more from the people around her.

After dinner the quartet that had been playing was replaced by a rock group, and the younger diners begin to file onto the dance floor. Addie turned in her chair to watch. Addie loved to dance, a fact that must have been obvious because it wasn't long before a tanned, muscular man beckoned to Addie from the dance floor. That was all the invitation she needed.

Booger, on Delilah's right, watched the couple for a while, then muttered, "He's got to be taking steroids."

He turned to Delilah. "Addie is acting really weird, Dee. Really weird. She's talking about her biological clock and being in her sexual prime and going around only once."

"There's nothing weird about that," Delilah said. "I think Addie is simply ready to settle down."

"She doesn't look settled," he grumbled, returning his gaze to the dance floor. "Do you think she's serious about wanting to get married?"

"Yes, I do. And I think it's exactly what she needs. Addie was made for marriage. She's a warm kind of person, the kind who shouldn't be alone."

"She's not alone. She has friends. She has me."

"You know and I know that friends don't take the place of a husband. Most women need more. Addie needs more. She needs someone who is just for her."

"You mean she's looking to get laid?"

"Among other things," Delilah said, hiding her smile at his obvious jealousy. "Isn't sex important to you?"

"Sure, but we're talking about Addie. Jeez, would you look at that idiot thrusting his crotch at her."

"Calm down. They're only dancing. Besides, Addie can't see a thing. She wouldn't know if he were thrusting a chain saw at her."

Booger grabbed Delilah's arm, his fingers digging into her flesh as he kept his gaze on Addie. "And she's jiggling her boobs at him! Where did Addie get boobs anyway?"

"She's always had them. Her new dress simply shows them off a little."

"I don't like it. I don't like it at all."

"Don't be such a prude. If she were jiggling them at you, you wouldn't be complaining."

He frowned. "No, I guess I wouldn't." With an abrupt movement he pushed his chair back and stalked out onto the dance floor, heading in Addie's direction.

It looked as though the plan was working out just fine. At least, it might if Addie noticed that her dance partner had changed.

Delilah needn't have worried. As soon as Booger reached Addie he took her into his arms, ignoring completely the young Adonis.

Great, Delilah thought with a wry smile. Wonderful. She had Addie's life under control. Why couldn't she do something about her own? She should have been having a fantastic time flirting with Steve, a man who was definitely ripe for a new relationship.

Bill, she thought, answering her own question. He had sent all her plans haywire. It wasn't fair that a casually met stranger should mess her up like no man had ever done before. She wouldn't let him get to her, she told herself stubbornly. She had to take control of her life again.

Until this conference was over, she would take care to stay well out of Bill Shelley's way.

Bill leaned over the bar and tapped the bartender on the shoulder. "Hit me again, Sam."

"I keep telling you my name is Winston," the slender bartender said as he refilled Bill's glass. "Don't you think you've had enough of this stuff?"

"I can handle it."

"I don't know," Winston said doubtfully. "Club soda affects some people real funny."

"What time is it?"

"It's two minutes later than the last time you asked." Winston glanced at his watch. "It's three and a half minutes past twelve. Isn't that a watch on your wrist?"

Bill nodded. "But if I keep looking at my watch I'll seem anxious. I'll look like I've been stood up."

"What time was she supposed to be here?"

"Ten."

"This is just a guess—I mean it's not like a scientific survey or anything—but I would say you have been stood up."

"Who asked you?" Bill muttered.

Why was he there, he asked himself silently. Why was he waiting for a woman who obviously was not coming? She probably didn't give a damn about him. She was probably dancing and laughing with a man one of the members of her precious group had found for her. She had probably forgotten a man named Bill Shelley existed.

"What time is it, Sam?"

"Twelve-oh-five. And she still ain't here."

"No, she still ain't here." He smiled slightly. "She said she wouldn't be here. I should accept that, shouldn't I? I should give it up and leave. That's exactly what I should do." He sighed. "Give me another drink, Sam."

"Judas Priest, Bill, you're gonna explode in a minute."

"That's what women do to you," Bill said glumly. "They twist you all up inside and make you drown your sorrows in club soda."

"You gonna cry, Bill?" Winston asked warily.

Bill laughed. "Not yet. Ask me again at twelve-thirty. Have you got a woman, Sam?"

"Naw, she ran off with a Toyota dealer. That's why I'm in Mexico instead of in Little Rock like the good Lord intended. I followed them and took one of his cars, a cute little red job. I figured it was a fair trade. The police didn't quite see it that way."

"Can the Toyota listen to your dreams and carry on an intelligent conversation?"

"No, but neither could Sally."

Bill leaned forward, poking Winston's thin chest to make his point. "Ah, but can a pile of metal keep your bed and your heart warm?"

The bartender leaned against the bar and sighed. "Sally had the damnedest little giggle. Made my toes curl every time I heard it."

Silence fell as each man was drawn into his own thoughts. Bill sat staring into his glass, remembering the way Lila had kissed him at the valley of the rainbows. She was cool on the outside, but beneath the surface there was a passionate heart. He had felt it then. He had felt it the first time he ever saw her.

She should have followed her passionate heart, he told himself. Or, if she couldn't follow her own, she should have followed his. He knew it was heading in the right direction. Instead, she had said she wouldn't meet him at the bar. She had said it very firmly.

But Bill was still there, and he was still waiting. He felt his whole life had been nothing more than time spent waiting for Lila. He could wait a while longer.

"What time is it, Sam?"

"Twelve-fifteen."

Bill slumped forward and ran his finger down the side of his glass. "How did she get inside me so quickly?" he murmured. "In my head . . . in my blood." He glanced up. "I guess I'd sound like a wuss if I said in my heart."

"Hey," Winston said, shaking his head, "you'd be surprised at some of the weird stuff a bartender hears. You wanna say she's in your heart, say it."

"She's in my heart," Bill said quietly. "Lila is in my heart. Why isn't she in my arms? Why isn't she in this damn bar?"

Winston stared over Bill's head toward the entrance to the room. "Is she blond with a figure that would stop an eighteen wheeler?"

Bill felt his heart skitter sideways, then it began to pound loudly enough for everyone in the room to hear. Slowly he swung around on the barstool until he was facing the door.

With her hands clenched at her sides, Delilah stood just inside the door of the dimly lit bar. She didn't know why she was there. She had developed a killer headache and had told her friends she was going to the suite.

Then suddenly she had found herself in the bar. And her headache was gone.

I should leave right now, she told herself. She should get out of there and back to sanity as quickly as possible.

But it was too late. Already Bill had slid off the

barstool and was walking toward her. Too late. Maybe it had been too late from the moment she met him.

When he reached her, he stood for a moment looking down at her. "I knew you'd come," he murmured.

"Did you?"

He shook his head. "No, I was lying. I didn't think you'd be here."

"Neither did I."

"Did that scare you as much as it did me?"

"Yes," she whispered, "I guess it did."

For a long time he simply stood there. Delilah could hear him breathing but he didn't say anything. Then without another word he took her hand, and together they walked out of the bar.

Behind them Delilah thought she heard someone say "Way to go, Bill . . . nice to meet you, Lila," but decided she must have imagined it.

Bill was staying in a small one-bedroom suite on the ground floor of the hotel. Country music was playing on the radio as they stepped inside the room. He left her side and walked to the radio, turning the dial quickly. He passed several Spanish stations, then suddenly the sounds of Chopin's Heroic Polonaise filled the room.

"That's better," he said, turning toward her. "It's triumphant music." He frowned. "Unless you'd rather have something else?"

Delilah glanced around the room, staring at a

huge basket of fruit on the coffee table as she tried to find something to do with her hands. Why didn't she smoke?

"Is the music important?"

" 'My baby left me for a trucker' didn't seem right somehow," he said. "And I want everything to be right." He gestured toward the coffee table. "Want some fruit? The avocados are great."

She turned her head and stared at him for a moment. Delilah had expected silky words and iced champagne. Those were the instruments of seduction, not Chopin and avocados.

"Bill, are you nervous?" Her voice sounded incredulous to her own ears.

"Petrified," he said without any sign of embarrassment. "How about you?"

She laughed, feeling a glow settle over her body. "I didn't know men got nervous about . . . you know."

He ran a hand through his already disheveled hair. "This is the first time I've ever been nervous about 'you know.' 'You know' doesn't usually throw me for a loop. It's you. I've met the perfect woman and I don't want to scare her off." He raised one thick brow. "You want to play checkers instead?"

She couldn't stop laughing. He was so damned cute.

His smile was crooked, his eyes sparkling as he watched her laughing face. After a moment he stepped closer, still staring, as though he couldn't bear to look away from her.

He picked up her hand, running his thumb

over her knuckles as he spoke. "I guess you know how I feel about you." He laughed softly. "I mean, I haven't exactly tried to hide it. I'm in love with you, Lila." Something must have shown on her face then, because he suddenly tightened his hold on her hand. "Don't panic. I know you don't feel the same way. That's all right. I just wanted you to understand. I knew the minute I saw you that you were the woman I've been waiting for." He put his arms around her, inhaling deeply as he buried his face in her neck. "I've been lonely for you, Lila," he whispered hoarsely.

Delilah felt reality dissolve around her. He loved her. This wonderful man loved her. And as she stood in the circle of his arms and felt his warm breath on her throat, it almost felt as though she belonged there. For the first time since she was fourteen, she felt as though she belonged.

It was so right, so overwhelmingly right.

Then suddenly a dark hole opened up, and Delilah fell through it. It wasn't right. It was very, very wrong. Bill wasn't in love with her. He was in love with nice, normal Lila Jones, the woman who didn't exist.

"Bill, wait," she whispered urgently. "Bill"—she turned her head away from his kiss—"listen to me. There are things you don't know, things you should know. About me." She pulled away from him and pushed her hair from her face with a rough hand. "You see . . . well, the thing is, I haven't told you everything." She gave a short laugh. "What am I talking about? I haven't told you anything."

He reached out and ran one finger gently down her cheek. "You can tell me anything, Lila. And I'll listen. But it won't make any difference. I already know all I need to know about you."

She stared at him, studying his face. Then she shook her head in bewilderment. "You really aren't interested, are you?"

"Wrong. I'm interested in everything about you. I'm simply saying that some things are inconsequential."

"But how do you know what I was going to tell you is inconsequential?"

He smiled. "Were you going to tell me you don't want to make love with me?"

"No," she said weakly, "not that."

"Then anything else is inconsequential. We can talk now or we can talk later." He ran one hand slowly over her hip. "I'd prefer later, but if you want to tell me now, I'll listen." He paused, giving her a look that was slightly wistful. "Can I kiss you first?"

She frowned at him. "Would you stop looking so damned adorable?"

"Yes, ma'am. I'll try." He moved his hands up her arms to her shoulders. "Was that what you wanted to tell me? Can I kiss you now?"

She sagged weakly under his touch. "You're making this extremely difficult. I can't keep my mind on what I was going to say."

He bent his head to press several kisses to her neck. "That makes two of us." He slid the zipper of the dress slowly downward. "I think you were saying something about not having told me everything."

"Yes, that's it."

He slid the dress off her shoulder and lowered his lips to the exposed flesh. His breathing was audibly more erratic. "So tell me, Lila. Tell me everything."

She tried to say something, anything. But she could only watch as he drew back and let her dress slide to the floor. Without taking his gaze from her, he began to unbutton the white shirt he wore beneath a tan jacket.

"Do you want to help me with this . . . while you tell me everything?" he asked softly.

She shook her head vehemently, her gaze glued to his chest. He shrugged out of his shirt and jacket with a single movement, then after a moment he reached out slowly and unhooked the front clasp of her bra.

When the clasp gave beneath his fingers, he exhaled and smiled. "I was afraid it wouldn't unhook. Then I would have looked like a fool. That's another one of those macho things I was—"

He broke off as Delilah reached up and spread the lace of her bra, sliding the straps off her shoulders.

"Sweet heaven," he breathed hoarsely. Grasping her arms, he pulled her close, moaning as her flesh met his. "Lila?" he whispered roughly.

"Yes?"

"Are we through talking?"

"Yes . . . yes, I believe we are."

"Good." He paused, trying to consume her throat and bare shoulders, then, "Lila?"

"Yes?"

"I find myself caught on the horns of a dilemma," he whispered. The words were muffled as he moved his attention to the back of her neck.

A tingling shiver spread through her, leaving goose bumps in its wake. "A horny dilemma?" she said weakly.

"Exactly. My mind is saying 'This lady is fragile. She needs lots of care, so go slowly and let her get used to the feel of you.' "

Delilah had never thought of herself as fragile. She was tough. She had had to be in order to survive. "That's what your mind is saying?"

"Yes." He groaned as she moved lightly against him. "But my body is saying 'If you don't get this lady into bed in the next three seconds, there's going to be *big* trouble.' "

"*Big* trouble?"

"Yeah, like California dropping into the ocean or the Rocky Mountains being flattened. That kind of trouble. My body is saying something catastrophic will happen if I don't make love to you now. Immediately."

As her head rested on his shoulder she could see her bright pink nails against the smooth skin of his back. She was fascinated by the erotic picture it made.

"Bill," she whispered finally, "as a doctor I can say only—listen to your body; it would never lie to you."

His arms tightened convulsively, squeezing the breath out of her. Then he laughed in triumph and picked her up in his arms. In the bedroom he fell across the bed, still holding her tightly.

"I want to eat you up," he said, his eyes blazing as he stared at her face. "I want to touch every part of you. I want to explore every inch of your body. I want to cram thirty-nine years of missing you into one night. But right now, more than anything, I want to be inside you. I want to feel you all around me. I really, really want that, Lila."

A breathless laugh caught in her throat. "I really, really want that too, Bill."

In the next few seconds Delilah braced herself for their coming together, wondering how she could want him so badly and still be so very afraid. This territory where he was about to take her was unknown. Because although Delilah knew all there was to know about sex, she knew absolutely nothing about making love.

Then before she could continue the thought, before the panic could build in her, he was there, and his arms were around her, and there was no room for fear, no room for pain. With unerring movements Bill became a part of her, and it was right. It was as though their bodies had been made specifically to be joined. As though no other possibility existed for either of them.

She was instantly bombarded with sensations, wilder and more beautiful than she had ever dreamed possible. Each movement, each caress, was like a silver thread that bound her to him, tighter and ever tighter, until she felt every emotion he felt, thought his thoughts, dreamed his dreams.

Gradually something began to build inside her, pulling her back into her own body. Although it was fiery, intense, and painfully sweet, she tried desperately to reject it. She didn't want to leave him to go off on her own. She didn't want to feel her own sensations, she wanted to feel his, she wanted to feel theirs.

Then suddenly she heard his voice close against her ear, whispering, "I'm with you, Lila. It's okay. Let it happen."

So she gave in to the sensation. And as it shook through her body, he was there just as he had promised, holding her, joining her in even this.

Long, long moments later, Delilah lay beside Bill, her exhausted body drenched in perspiration, her eyes wide open, her mind stunned.

She couldn't take it all in. The thoroughly nice, sweet man had suddenly become a tiger. He hadn't been brutal, but he most certainly hadn't been hesitant. He had been so passionate, so sensual, so giving, she had wanted to scream with the intensity of the pleasure.

It had been a truly remarkable night. It had been a night Delilah knew she would remember for as long as she lived. Because when Bill had held her and made love to her she had felt complete. For one night she had felt whole again.

Seven

"*I love you, Lila,*" the young ghost said. "*Do you love me back?*"

"*Yes, Buddy, I love you back.*"

"*But not just 'cause I'm your brother?*"

"*No, I love you because you're a silly squirrel. And because you're ticklish . . . right here.*"

The childish laughter rang loud. Then, though Delilah tried to hold on to it, it faded away and was replaced by a different voice.

"*I love you, Dee-Dee,*" the phantom said raspily. "*Be still and quiet and let me show you how much I love you.*"

"*Don't. You can't. Please don't. Please!*"

Silent terror filled the world and lingered even as the last spirit appeared.

"*How could you do this to me?*" the wraith shrieked. "*My own daughter. I loved you. My God, I loved you, and you're nothing but filth!*"

"*No, Mama. Don't say those things. Mama, I'm sorry. I'm so sorry . . .*"

Delilah's eyes opened abruptly, her heart pounding painfully, her body drenched in perspiration. After a disoriented moment she pulled herself up to lean against the headboard.

She hadn't had the dream in years. It was the same as always, coming to her in the nether world that lay between sleep and consciousness, seeming more real than any dream produced by normal sleep.

It had been so long since the last time, she had hoped she was rid of it. Why had it returned now?

Glancing around the room, she realized she was back in the suite she shared with the group. As she came more fully awake, Delilah remembered leaving Bill's room in the early hours of the morning, moving carefully and silently so that she wouldn't wake him.

Bill. Without warning, memories of the night before washed over her, leaving her weak and breathless. She relived the feel of his hands on her, her hands on him. His scent and the warmth of his flesh. The memory alone brought stronger emotion than Delilah had ever allowed herself to feel.

And that was why the nightmare had returned, she told herself. Bill, with his loving heart and passionate hands, had brought her back to life. For years all her emotions had been carefully buried, but in Bill's arms she had begun to feel again. And she was once more open to the pain—past, future, and present.

Scrambling out of bed, she dressed quickly and

quietly. She didn't want to wake Addie. She wanted to be out of the hotel before any of her friends awakened. Before Bill awakened.

An hour later Delilah stepped aboard a crowded pleasure boat. As she mingled with the other tourists, finding the anonymity she needed in the crowd, she allowed her thoughts to return to what had happened the night before. She allowed herself to think about Bill.

He had said he loved her. Bill had said he loved her. She still couldn't believe it. Things like that didn't happen to Delilah Jones. Not that she hadn't heard the words before. She had. Dozens of times. But she had always known that the words were nothing more than a man's way of telling her that he wanted her body in his bed or her beauty at his side. No one had ever tried to look inside her and love the real Delilah Jones.

Closing her eyes, Delilah didn't even try to fight the wave of self-contempt that swept over her. She was mooning around, thinking of how last night had felt from her side. What she had avoided looking at was what Bill had felt. And what he would feel when she told him the truth.

She had let it go on too long, she acknowledged silently. She had willfully allowed a sweet, harmless flirtation to become complicated. Although she knew Bill wasn't really in love with her, he believed he was. And that meant he was going to get hurt.

Sweet heaven, she hadn't wanted that. She had intended to put an end to everything before that could happen.

Although she tried, she couldn't find it in her to regret their lovemaking. It had been too wonderful. But she should have told him the truth first. She should have insisted on telling him who and what she was. Dammit, she should have found a way.

But she hadn't. It had been pitifully easy for him to convince her that explanations could wait until later. Like the selfish witch she was, she had grabbed what he was offering with both hands. She had wanted his love. She had been greedy for it. She had wanted to pretend that she had a right to it. Lord help her, she had wanted to pretend that last night was a beginning for them.

What a joke, she thought, leaning her head wearily against the side of the boat. It would take a mind more ingenious than hers to imagine hardhearted Delilah Jones with a sweet man like Bill.

Even if he really loved her—her, not the woman she had created—Delilah knew it would never have worked. Bill should have a woman who was clean and whole, a woman who wasn't all twisted inside, a woman who could love him as he deserved to be loved.

Gradually, bit by bit throughout the day, memories of the beauty she had found with Bill began to fade, and the darkness and doubts returned. It wasn't a pleasant experience, but it was familiar. It was something she had had years of practice at handling. It was reality.

Hours later Delilah walked along the beach toward the hotel. The sun had already set and it was that peaceful time between day and night.

She hadn't wanted to come back, but she knew she couldn't spend the rest of her time in Acapulco avoiding Bill. Sooner or later she would have to see him and tell him the truth, about her character and about her past. She had to make him understand what she was. And then it would be over.

Simple, painful reality.

With a shake of her head she stubbornly picked up her pace. There was no sense in putting off the inevitable.

On her left, a few yards away, she saw a woman sitting alone on the beach near the edge of the water. Delilah almost passed her before she realized it was Glory.

Delilah walked over and sat down on the sand beside her friend. After a moment Glory turned her head, belatedly acknowledging Delilah's presence. "Where did you disappear to?" Her voice was strangely flat. "Addie's been looking everywhere for you."

"I needed some time alone."

When Glory made no effort to continue the conversation, Delilah studied the younger woman's face carefully. Catching her breath at the undisguised sorrow there. This must be what Addie had seen.

"The whole world is changing," Delilah said in confusion. "This was supposed to be such a wonderful vacation. All of us together again after so long. What's happened to us?"

Glory bit her lip, turning her face toward the ocean. She was silent for a long time, then she began to speak quietly. "You know, Dee, when I found Alan I didn't want to believe in what we had. I think I was afraid to believe. See, if it was real, then I could lose it. For the first six months of our marriage this . . . this fear nagged at me constantly. It was always there, just below the surface. My life with Alan was so beautiful. So damned beautiful."

Glory drew in a shaky breath. "You have to pay for that kind of happiness, Dee. Sooner or later you have to pay."

Delilah was suddenly scared for her friend. Something had gone terribly terribly wrong for her. "Tell me," she whispered hoarsely.

Glory didn't answer for a moment. She tried to smile, but her lips trembled, ruining it. "I can't have children, Dee. I can't ever have children." She closed her eyes tightly. "I wanted Alan's baby." She drew the back of her hand roughly across her cheeks to wipe away the dampness. "I wanted it so much."

"Are you sure?" Delilah said, feeling a painful tightness in her chest. "This is the age of medical miracles. Have you gotten a second opinion?"

"Second and third and fourth." Her voice was bitter, final.

"I'm sorry," Delilah said quietly. "How is Alan taking it?"

Glory sighed. "Alan has been wonderful. I didn't think it was possible, but he's been even more loving than before."

"Then you have a lot more than most people

ever get, Glory," Delilah said, more roughly than she had intended. "Can't you be satisfied with that?"

Glory kept her head turned away as she whispered, "Dee, he wants a baby. I know he does. Don't you see? This is something that he wants so badly, and I can't give it to him. I'll never be able to give it to him. When we're together we pretend. We pretend that we don't mind so much. We pretend that everything is fine. And the pretense is growing into a solid wall between us."

"Maybe the wall's only in your mind. Maybe Alan's not pretending. Isn't it just possible that you really are all he needs?"

"He said—" The words were a rough whisper. She swallowed and began again. "He said we could adopt."

Delilah swore long and hard, pulling up every vulgarity she had ever heard to vocalize her anger. Damn him, she thought. Damn him to hell.

Apparently Alan wasn't as smart as Delilah had thought he was. Didn't the idiot know that now was not the time to talk about adoption, she asked herself silently. Maybe sometime in the future, but not now. Not when Glory was grieving for her child, the child she would never have.

Drawing in a deep, steadying breath, Delilah said, "Why don't you talk to him? You need to let him know what you're feeling."

Glory nodded apathetically. "I will . . . sometime." She smiled. "I'll be okay, Dee. You know me. I always bounce back."

Glory returned her gaze to the water, resting her chin on her knees. After a while Delilah stood up and, without another word, walked away. There was nothing more she could say.

That was what love got you, Delilah told herself, kicking at the sand in anger. Pain and more pain. She had hoped Glory was immune. She should have known better. No one was immune. Love, the universal destroyer.

Delilah had just reached the terrace when Alan walked out of the hotel. Spotting her, he waved and hurried toward her, but Delilah simply nodded as she walked past him.

Alan grabbed her arm and smiled. "What's up?" When she didn't answer, his smile faded. Furrows appeared on his brow as he gave Delilah a puzzled look. "Have you seen my darling? She's done a disappearing act."

Delilah hesitated, then, turning away from his gaze, she said, "I've seen her, but I think she wants to be alone right now, Alan."

When his hand tightened on her arm, Delilah glanced at him. He looked grim suddenly, like the dark pirate Glory had called him shortly after they had first met. "Where is she, Dee?"

She jerked her arm away. "I said she wants to be alone. Dammit, haven't you done enough already? Just leave her alone."

"What are you talking about?"

Delilah ran a hand through her hair. It was none of her business. She should stay out of it completely.

But she couldn't. "Why did you have to mention adoption?" she asked, allowing her anger to show at last. "Couldn't you see, couldn't you sense that she's in mourning? It was a stupid, stupid thing to do."

Alan jerked back as though she had struck him. But Delilah couldn't stop. "You promised me four years ago that you would keep her safe and happy," she told him. "Damn, Alan, I trusted you. She trusted you. If you can't protect her from this kind of hurt, you don't deserve her."

She glared at him, then looked away from the deep pain in his dark eyes. After a moment she let out a slow breath. Damn him. "She's on the beach," she said shortly.

With clenched fists she watched Alan run down the beach toward Glory. And Delilah felt a strange sensation, as though she, too, were being watched.

Whirling around, she found Bill sitting in a chair beside a flowering bush. His eyes were narrowed slightly as he studied her intently.

"What in hell are you staring at?" she demanded, her voice harsh. "I tried to tell you last night. I tried to tell you I'm not that nice, special woman you keep talking about. Maybe now you'll believe me." She turned and began walking quickly toward the hotel.

Seconds later he caught up with her, grasping her arm to swing her around to face him. One look at his face made Delilah go weak in the knees. When she began to shake, he pulled her into his arms, stroking her hair as he whispered incomprehensible words of comfort.

"Why?" she asked hoarsely against his neck. "Why are you treating me like this when I'm such a bitch?"

"You're not a bitch, love. You were just worried about a friend."

She stepped away from him, shaking her head wildly. "Don't do that. Don't build fairy tales around me, Bill. I'm not who you think I am. I don't know how to be that person. I told you that you have no idea who or what I am."

He shoved his hands into his pockets, his shoulders slightly slumped. "And I told you that I do know you. I know you've been hurt and have built walls to protect yourself. I know you're beautiful inside and out. Maybe I don't know where you've been or where you're going, but I know you. I knew who you were the minute I saw you." He smiled his crooked smile. "I looked into your eyes and I knew you were the woman who was made especially for me." He moved his shoulders in a faint shrug. "That may not be what you want to hear, Lila, but it's the truth."

As Delilah stared at him she suddenly realized why he had seemed familiar from the very beginning. It was the trusting look of adoration she saw in his eyes. It was the same look she had seen in Buddy's eyes so many years before. And now she felt the same urgent need to protect Bill that she had felt toward her brother.

Moving away, she stood with her back to him. "This time you're going to listen to the truth," she said, her voice determined. "All this time, since the first minute we met, I've been pretending, Bill. You're a nice man, and I knew we wouldn't see each other again when we leave here so I decided to pretend to be a nice, normal woman. It was all a game . . . just a silly game."

She turned slowly to face him, then stopped. He was smiling. Smiling as though he knew something she didn't.

"Damn!" she said in frustration. "Listen to me. I *lied* to you. There were no loving parents, no suburban background, no happy childhood. None of that was true. What I didn't borrow from Addie's life, I made up. I was taking you for a ride."

"I know," he said quietly.

She stiffened. "What do you mean, you know?"

"You made too many mistakes. You kept changing your father's age and your mother's hobbies and— Don't you see? It doesn't matter. None of that is important. Your background isn't all that makes you Lila."

He didn't understand yet, she told herself wearily. But he would. She would make sure of it.

Speaking slowly and deliberately, she said, "By the time I was fourteen I was on my own, living in the streets. Things"—she stopped to clear her throat—"bad things happen when you live on the street."

He drew in a sharp breath. "*Why?* Why were you alone? Why were you on the streets? Sweet heaven, baby, how did you survive?"

"None of that matters. What matters is that on the street you learn to lie and steal and cheat. I've

done it all. But that's not the worst I've done."
She turned her head and looked him squarely in
the eye. "I've slept with only one other man before
you. That was when I was sixteen. I—" She broke
off and swallowed the painful lump in her throat.
"I didn't sleep with him because I loved him or
even because I wanted him. I let him . . . I let him
use me so that I would have a safe place to sleep.
Just for one night. I wanted to be secure and
unafraid for just one night."

Her smile was bitter as she stared at him.
"Whether you take money or a safe bed, selling it
is selling it." Her voice dropped to a harsh, barely
audible whisper. "Do you know what that makes
me?"

For a long time there was only silence. Just
when she thought she would have to scream or go
crazy, he said, "Yes, I know what that makes
you." The words sounded gentle. So incredibly
gentle. "It makes you human. It makes you a
survivor. Don't put ugly labels on what happened
to you. I was in Vietnam. I saw what the children
there—some of them not more than babies—had
to do simply to stay alive. Do you think I thought
any less of them for it?"

He still didn't understand, she told herself, feeling suddenly frantic. He refused to understand.

"How old are you, Lila?"

She glanced up sharply in confusion. "Thirty-
four," she said finally.

A strange look crossed his features, a look of
wonder and awe. "Eighteen years," he whispered

with a painful catch in his voice. "Dear Lord, Lila, *eighteen years*. And in all that time you've never wanted a man. But you wanted *me*. *You want me*."

"*Stop it!*" she screamed at him, wrapping her arms tightly around her waist. "You still don't get it, do you? You're too damn nice to understand. Too damn good. You're the kind of man they kill off in a disaster movie so the audience can have a good cry."

She drew air deeply into her lungs, searching for a calmness she couldn't quite find. "You're trying to make it sound romantic, and it just won't work. Let me tell you the truth about your precious Lila. After I got off the streets, after I fought my way back to the civilized world, I didn't just forget all I had learned. It doesn't happen that way in real life. You don't suddenly become a new person simply because your environment changes."

She grasped his arm, giving him a slight shake. "Bill, listen to me. I'm what men call a tease— that's one of the more polite terms they use. I've heard them all, and I deserved them all. I make men want me, then I don't come through. I use their desire for me to get my kicks. To make me feel powerful. To make me feel in control. Now do you understand?"

He stared at her for a moment, his head tilted slightly to one side. "I understand that you're telling me these things to try to put me off," he said quietly. "What I don't understand is why."

I'm telling you these things because I'm scared, she thought in desperation. More scared than she had been in those terrible years she was living on the streets. More scared than when her mother died. She was scared because she felt too much for this man. She had promised herself she would never feel this much again.

Bill reached out and touched her face. "It didn't work, Lila. You haven't put me off. For heaven's sake, do you know what it means to me, knowing that I'm the first man in your life? I'm not talking about virginity. I don't give a damn about that. I'm talking about the important things, your mind and your heart. I'm the first man you've trusted with the truth. I'm the first man you've willingly given yourself to."

He cupped her cheek, turning her face toward him. "Don't you see? You were waiting for me, Lila. Only for me."

It was crazy. She knew it was crazy, so how could he make it sound so reasonable? There were a thousand objections she should be making, but she couldn't think of even one at the moment. She couldn't think of anything as long as Bill was touching her.

Closing her eyes tightly, Delilah allowed a little of the darkness to slip away.

After a moment he slid his arm around her waist and walked with her to a wicker love seat. When they were seated, he began rubbing her hands, as though she were the swooning heroine of a Victorian novel. The laugh that caught in her throat was only slightly cynical.

"I missed you today," he said gently. "I missed you when I woke up and you weren't there beside me like you were supposed to be. Then I couldn't find you anywhere. I saw Addie, but she didn't know where you were either."

"I went out on a boat. I don't remember a thing about it. I guess I missed you too," she admitted reluctantly. "I would be going along, feeling all dark and miserable because I knew I was going to have to tell you about myself—my past. Then suddenly I would think of last night and avocados and Chopin, and I would find myself smiling." She was smiling at him in that same way now. "How can I work up a decent depression if you keep making me smile?"

He leaned down and kissed her, his mouth moving on hers hungrily. Then suddenly he pulled back a fraction of an inch and raised one thick brow. "The kind of guy they kill off in disaster movies?" he asked in disbelief.

Delilah laughed, and the tension in her began to ease away. It felt good to be sitting beside him, talking of unimportant things. It felt good to laugh again. She had had enough intensity for one day.

"Delilah. Yo, Delilah!"

At the shouted words they both glanced around and saw Addie feeling her way across the terrace. "Delilah, is that you?" she asked a potted fern. "I know I heard your voice. Dee, please, I need help!"

"Addie dear," Delilah called to her. "Listen carefully, and I'll tell you one more time. We water plants, we talk to people."

"Dee!"

Addie stumbled toward the sound of Delilah's voice, and Bill stood as she drew nearer.

"Thank God I found you," she said, sounding breathless, as though she had been running. "You didn't tell me what to do next. I've done the kiss thing a couple of thousand times. We're both getting chapped lips. I left Booger out there"—she waved a vague hand in the direction of the beach —"in a gazebo. I just said wait a minute and left him. Dee, what in hell am I supposed to do now?"

Bill put both hands on Addie's shoulders to steady her. "Calm down, Addie."

"Bill?" she said, squinting up at him. "I thought you were a tree."

"I'm not," he assured her.

"Dee," Addie said, her voice frantic, "we forgot to work out something for after the kiss part. What's next? What's my strategy?"

Bill chuckled, shaking his head. "Forget strategy. You don't need anyone's help." He leaned down and kissed her cheek. "Trust your instincts, Addie. Don't ask questions, just do what comes next."

"You're sure? Dee?"

"Go for it, Addie," Delilah said, smiling at Bill.

Addie inhaled, straightened her blouse, and, looking eager, said, "Right. Go for it," then walked away.

"Nice lady," Bill said.

"Weird lady," Delilah corrected him as Addie ran into a chaise longue and crawled across it without slowing down. "She's in love with Booger."

"I'm glad. I want everyone to be happy tonight." He smiled at her. "As happy as I am."

She studied his loving features, then frowned slightly. "Bill— "

"Shhh," he said, shaking his head at her. "Don't worry about the future. Don't think about what's going to happen tomorrow or the tomorrow after that. For now let's just get to know each other. Let's just be together." He grinned. "What could it hurt?"

Bill knew the truth about her now. At least, he knew a good deal of it, she amended silently. He knew the worst of it. He knew, and he still wanted her. If Delilah believed in miracles, this would have felt like one.

The smile she gave him was only slightly shaky. "What could it hurt?" she repeated softly.

Eight

Delilah lay motionless, her eyes barely open. It was early, in the special hours when the world still had a fuzzy edge to it, before the sun brought everything into focus. The dream had come to her again at the moment of awakening. But now, feeling Bill's warmth beside her, it didn't matter so much. The pain seemed distant.

Pushing the cover aside, she ran her hands slowly over her stomach and thighs, then over her arms and shoulders.

Bill shifted slightly. "What are you doing?"

His voice, husky with sleep, made her feel warm and melty, like a Hershey bar that had been left out in the sun. She would have never believed how incredibly intimate a man's sleepy voice could sound.

Bill's voice, she corrected herself silently with a tiny secret smile.

He raised himself up on one elbow to look down

at her. "You obviously haven't looked closely enough at your job description," he said after a moment. "It goes like this—I touch your body, you touch mine."

She laughed softly. "I'm feeling the differences in my body," she explained. "It's changed."

She brought her hands to her breasts. They felt fuller and more a part of her than they had before. Glancing down, she saw a small bruise high on her left breast. The memory of how it came to be there brought a sweet rush of pleasure.

He moved her hand away with his own and cupped her breast, leaning down to kiss the bruise. "I monogrammed you," he murmured. "This says William Walter Shelley."

"Monogrammed?" she repeated, finding it difficult to look down her nose at him from a reclining position. Difficult but not impossible. "Monogrammed, as in handkerchiefs or a bathrobe? As in your underwear when you go away to camp?"

He gave her a slow grin. "Yeah, like that. Like a silk shirt. Something personal that I keep *real* close to my body."

"I see," she said slowly, sitting up and rolling him onto his stomach.

"What are you doing?" He raised his head to peer at her over his shoulder.

"I'm simply sticking to my job description," she said, rising to her knees beside him. "Remember? You touch my body, I touch yours."

"I don't trust you," he said, his eyes narrowed slightly. "You're planning retribution of some kind."

When she kissed the back of his neck, then blew gently on the soft fuzz, he said, "Mmmmm, I still don't trust you." Then when she moved her lips to his shoulders, "Ohhhh, yes, you're planning something devious, all right."

As Delilah kissed her way down to his lower back, he moved sensually under her lips, groaning softly.

"Trust me now?" she asked as she teased his warm flesh with her lips and tongue.

His breathing was heavier, almost distressed. "Hmm?" His voice sounded somewhat distracted.

"I asked if you trust me now?"

"Lord, yes."

"You shouldn't." She quickly moved down to one firm buttock and sank her teeth in.

He yelped loudly, then began to laugh. "Okay, you've had your revenge." He tried to reach her with his left hand, but she stayed just out of range. Still laughing, he said, "You've proved your point, Lila . . . *Lila.*"

She opened her mouth and kissed the spot before sitting back on her heels. "Monogrammed," she said in satisfaction. "It says Delilah Susan Jones"—she touched the teeth marks on his derriere—"right here."

In one move Bill turned and grabbed her, pulling her down beside him. His patchwork eyes were shining brightly with amusement. "You're wicked," he said, chuckling. "Absolutely wicked and absolutely wonderful."

Delilah wrapped her arms around him and

laughed with him. She had never known, never imagined, that the sexual part of life could be fun. Exciting, beautiful, and intense, but also fun.

How could she, she asked herself silently. Fun had died along with Buddy. Fun never hung out on the streets. How could she have envisioned herself finding joy in simply being alive? Because of Bill.

She reached up to touch his face, running one finger over the dimple in his left cheek. All because of Bill.

They made love again because they couldn't be in each other's arms and not make love, and afterward they made detailed, devious plans on how Delilah could sneak away from her friends to spend the day alone with Bill.

When she tiptoed into the suite it was still early. She stealthily checked Jack and Booger's room and found both beds empty, which meant the two mad doctors were somewhere on the loose, and she would have to take care avoiding them.

In the other bedroom she glanced quickly at Addie's bed. There was a gnarly lump in the middle, completely covered by a blanket.

Addie must have had a rough night, Delilah thought with a grin as she stripped down to her bra and panties. She hoped her friend had found something really special.

Like you did? a taunting voice in her head asked.

"Stop that!" she whispered. "It's not the same thing at all."

The lump in Addie's bed suddenly groaned. "Son of a gun, Dee, will you cut out the yelling?"

That was definitely not Addie's voice.

"God bless America, my head feels like it's been Osterized," the lump said, then moaned pathetically.

She walked to the bed and yanked back the cover.

Jack winced at the light, then made a pathetic gurgling sound. "Deeee, have a little pity."

She dropped the cover back over his head. "When did you turn into a whiner? And why are you in my bedroom?"

"Mine got a little crowded," he mumbled through the blanket. "I can handle kinky, but watching Booger and Addie make love would be like watching Bambi and . . . what was the girl deer's name—Flower?"

"I think that was the skunk. So Addie and Booger finally discovered—"

"Sex."

"—each other," she finished, smiling.

Love wasn't for her, but if this was what Addie wanted, Delilah was pleased for her. She began to move away from the bed, then suddenly turned back and yanked the cover down again. "Jack, how old are you?"

"Thirty," he said, pressing his hands tightly to his eyes to shut out the light. "If you're testing me to see if I still have human intelligence, don't waste your time. I think I left my IQ at a place called Maria's Hellhole."

"You're only four years younger than I am," she

said, sitting on the bed beside him. "Why are you still acting like the wild child?"

He spread his fingers slightly to look at her. "You're thirty-four? You don't look it. I thought you were Glory's age." He dropped his gaze to her lace-covered breasts. "You've certainly held together well."

"Answer my question. Why are you still playing games with alcohol?"

"None of your damn business."

He had visibly withdrawn from her. This wasn't the Jack Takara she knew from the old days. Back then he had had the world on a string. Everything had been fun and games to him. But he was serious now. Deadly serious.

First Addie, then Glory, now Jack, she thought broodingly. It looked as though the group had finally been forced into the unpleasant world of adulthood.

"What happened, Jack?" she asked quietly. "What's gone wrong for you since we were together in Dallas?"

"Life, Dee." His voice was more cynical than she had ever heard it. "That's what happened and that's what's gone wrong. There's a hole in the bucket, dear Liza, dear Liza," he said bitterly. "There's a hole in the bucket, dear Liza . . . a gaping damn hole."

"And you can't fix it? Is it your job at the hospital?" Jack's hospital had all the most modern equipment available. It was exactly the place Delilah would have chosen for him.

He didn't respond immediately. For a long time he leaned against the headboard, staring up at the ceiling. Then he said, "I'm going to tell you something I've never told anyone . . . never thought I would tell anyone. I'm only telling you because my brain is mucus this morning."

She nodded, waiting.

"I hate being a surgeon," he whispered. "I *despise* being a surgeon." He banged his head twice on the headboard, then winced and closed his eyes. "It's not what I wanted. I did it for my parents. So the old people could say 'my son the surgeon.' I thought I could hack it. I really thought I could. But it's getting so I have to force myself to get up in the morning." He covered his face with his hands. "Dee, I'm thirty years old. What in hell am I going to do?"

"What do you want to do?"

He shook his head weakly. "I don't know. I haven't thought about it. I've been too busy thinking about how much I hate surgery." He paused, shaking his head again. "Maybe research. I don't have Booger's brain, but I think I would be good at it."

"It would mean going back to school."

"That doesn't matter. The universities are where the really exciting work is being done right now . . . DNA. And viruses—my God, have I got ideas for viral research." The light that had grown steadily in his eyes suddenly went out. "That's crazy. How can I start over now? And even if I could, how in hell could I tell the old people?"

Delilah didn't know how to answer him. So she did the only thing she could do. She put her arms around Jack and held him tightly. It was something she wouldn't have dreamed of doing three years ago. Three days ago!

But like it or not, Delilah had changed. Willingly or not, she had become involved with life and the people around her. She cared.

Jack leaned his head on her shoulder for just a moment. When he pulled away, the old Jack was back—almost. Delilah knew it would never be quite the same between them.

"Thirty-four?" he said, then grinned slyly at her. "According to my calculations, you should be at your sexual peak in approximately three minutes. The bed is narrow, but that only makes it more interesting."

Delilah moved just as he lunged at her. Standing over him, she gave him the haughty look he expected from her. Then they both laughed.

Before Delilah stepped out of the elevator, she surveyed the lobby quickly, checking for booby traps. Booger and Addie, the diabolical duo, were out there somewhere, waiting to pounce on her. If Delilah could make it across the lobby to the door opening onto the terrace, she would be home free.

She almost made it. She was two steps away from the glass door when Glory appeared out of nowhere and grabbed her arm. "Delilah, wait up. I have something really exciting to tell you."

Delilah smiled ruefully. At least it was Glory, the sane one. Suddenly Delilah remembered everything that happened the evening before. The scene with Alan seemed like something from the distant past. All the sweetness of Bill lay between now and then.

"And I need to apologize," Delilah said, grimacing. "I shouldn't have said all those things to Alan last night. He probably hates me."

"Don't be silly." Glory smiled enigmatically. "We both love you dearly. Because of you, Alan and I talked. You were right, Dee. And I couldn't have been more wrong. I was torturing myself for nothing." She paused, then said quietly, "I don't know what we're going to do—I mean about having children. Alan mentioned adoption for me, not for him. But I just don't know. I know only that whatever happens, Alan and I are together, and that's all that matters."

Glory gave her head a slight shake. "This is not what I wanted to talk to you about." She paused dramatically. "Dee, we did it. Alan and I did it."

"Most married couples do," Delilah said, raising one slender brow. "But they don't usually go around telling all and sundry."

Glory laughed. "That's not what I meant. Alan and I have found your man. I get the prize," she said gleefully. "Not only is this man a doctor, he's the keynote speaker, which means he's someone very important. Alan is bringing him along to meet you."

Delilah bit her lip. She wasn't interested in

seeing anyone except Bill. He was out there now, waiting for her on the terrace. Waiting for her. She would have to make her excuses quickly. Maybe if she . . .

At that moment Alan came into view. And the man walking at his side was Bill.

"Dr. Delilah Jones," Alan said when they reached the two women, "I'd like you to meet Dr. William Shelley."

"Dr. Jones," Bill said, reaching out to pull her into his arms. "Good to meet you."

Bill dipped his head and kissed her, hard. He smoothed his fingers over her buttocks, cupping them as he brought her body close to his. Delilah melted against him, returning the kiss eagerly. How could she do otherwise? These were Bill's arms, Bill's lips.

After a long, heated moment, she pulled back a fraction of an inch. "Dr. Shelley." Her husky voice was openly, outrageously sensual. "I can't tell you how pleased I am to meet you. Very, *very* pleased."

Glory glanced at Alan. "I have a feeling we missed something."

Alan smiled and put his arm around his wife. "I wouldn't be a bit surprised."

Seconds later Booger and Addie appeared from the direction of the coffee shop, dragging a man between them.

Bill, his arms still around Delilah, glanced at the newcomers and smiled. "Hello, Booger . . . Addie. I'm afraid you're too late. It's me."

"You?" Booger said. "Who found you?"

"Alan and I did," Glory told him. "Which means I won. You can bow anytime you like."

Addie turned to Booger, speaking around the man who still stood dazed and helpless between them. "I told you someone-whose-name-we-won't-mention was all wrong. Why don't you ever listen to me?"

Booger frowned, furrows appearing in his forehead. "Wait a minute. Just hold on. I really don't think this is legal. Alan's only an honorary member of the group. I'm almost positive that makes him ineligible. Let's find Jack and check this thing out."

"We're from Texas, a community property state," Alan said smugly. "That means we share everything, including Glory's title as superior member of the group. If you want to talk about legality, what about—"

Bill took Delilah's arm, and they began to casually ease away from the group, walking slowly until they were certain that no one had noticed. Then they ran.

Outside the hotel he pulled her into his arms and whirled her around. "Feel that? That's freedom, lady. We're free at last."

She laughed, then nipped his chin with her teeth. "Why didn't you tell me you were the keynote speaker? Glory says you're someone important. Are you?"

He shrugged. "I didn't think so, but I guess I am," he said, smiling. "After all, the conference coordinators sent me a basket of fruit . . . and God sent me you."

After a moment of total silence she punched him in the shoulder. "Will you please stop saying things that make me go all sappy?"

"Turnabout's fair play. I look at you and go sappy." He inhaled deeply. "Now, are you ready for an entire day of unadulterated top-of-the-line fun?"

After renting a car, Bill and Delilah drove to the nearby La Quebrada cliffs to see the divers, young lean men who plunged more than a hundred feet into the water of a rocky cove below. The divers had to time their falls exactly because the small cove was shallow except when the waves surged in.

The crowd of tourists was like a single entity that held its breath when it saw a dark-skinned body poised at the top of the cliff, then when the diver plunged, arms spread like a featherless bird, the audience exhaled in wonder and relief.

It was thrilling to watch, but, for Bill, not nearly as thrilling as watching Delilah, sharing her excitement, sharing her happiness.

After leaving La Quebrada, they spent the rest of the day simply wandering the streets of Acapulco, going where impulse took them, finding excitement and pleasure everywhere they turned. Twice they caught glimpses of Booger and Addie in the crowd of tourists and had to duck out of sight until the danger had passed.

Throughout the day Bill kept his eyes on Delilah. There was nothing he could ask for that gave him more pleasure. He wanted to watch her for the rest of his life. He wanted to watch her and hold her and make her happy.

Her past was like an ever-present pain in his gut. The night before, after they had gone to his room, she had played down what she had been through in those years on the streets, but he knew they must have been a living hell for her.

Occasionally Bill treated kids who lived on the street, the runaways and the castaways. They were always looking over their shoulders, their eyes haunted and haunting, always suspicious of anyone they came in contact with. The thought that Lila had been one of those desperate children ate at him. It was no wonder she was so wary now.

His love had missed the carefree excitement of her teenage years. She had missed the laughter, the giddiness.

Today he wanted to make it up to her, if only a little. For this day he wanted to give back part of what had been stolen from her.

Delilah lay in Bill's arms, staring at the dark ceiling as she listened to the gentle rhythm of his breathing. The warmth of their lovemaking was still with her, and she didn't want to lose it. She didn't want to fall asleep, knowing that sooner or later the dream would return.

All those ghosts, she thought, shivering slightly. All those poor, tortured ghosts.

When Bill felt her shiver, his arms tightened

around her. "I know you're not cold," he said. "What's wrong?"

"I thought you were asleep."

"And that made you shiver?"

She laughed softly. "No, silly. I guess a goose must have walked across my grave."

He was silent for a moment. He had to get her to talk. He wanted—he desperately needed—her to share everything with him. "Lila, please?"

"It's nothing, Bill. Nothing at all." She turned in his arms so that she was facing him. "Sometimes, just before I come fully awake, I have a dream that is not too pleasant."

"Tell me about it."

She shook her head in a movement that was negative and final. "The dream is about problems from the past. Old problems that really don't matter anymore."

"They matter if they still bother you. Share your dream with me, sweetheart," he said urgently. "Split up all the pain you've been carrying around so long and give me half, then it won't be so heavy for you."

Delilah framed his face with her hands, rubbing her thumb across his strong lips. "Have I ever told you what a dear, sweet man you are?"

"Add irresistible and relentlessly virile to that and you can tell me later. Right now I want to hear about the dream," he said stubbornly.

"There's not all that much to tell. The dream is nothing more than pieces of conversations," she said, her voice calm as though it really didn't matter. "Three ghosts from the past, coming back to relive memories. Memories of love."

"Love," she repeated, shuddering. And this time the word sounded like a vulgarity.

"Tell me."

She sighed and gave a short nod. "Buddy is always there first," she began quietly, "telling me that he loves me, asking if I love him." She shifted slightly in his arms. "You see, Buddy was born after my father left us, and Mama was . . . well, she was weak and always seemed to be off in a world of her own. So Buddy and I had only each other. He was my responsibility—and there was nothing I could do to stop him from dying. I was totally helpless."

She shook her head restlessly. "In the dream he asks me if I love him, and it feels like an accusation. I loved him, but I let him die."

"How did he die?"

"Cerebrospinal meningitis."

Bill swore softly. He knew what the disease was like, knew what seeing it must have done to her.

"By the time we realized how ill he was and got him to the hospital it was too late," she said, her voice dull. "I told my friends, the group, that I wanted to be a doctor for the money, and that was true, but it was only part of the truth. Mostly I wanted to be a doctor because of how helpless I felt when Buddy died. I didn't want to ever be that helpless again."

She fell silent, but the air between them was taut with the things she had not yet said. Bill knew there was more, much more. Somehow he had to make her let go of it all. Her dream was coming between them, and he couldn't allow anything to do that.

"The other ghosts?"

She laughed shortly. "You really are a glutton for punishment." She sighed. "The next voice is—"

When Delilah broke off abruptly, Bill could feel her trying to withdraw from him mentally, emotionally, and physically. He knew he was taking a big chance, forcing this on her, but he could see no other way.

"Lila, the next voice," he demanded.

"When I was ten and Buddy was four, Mama married a man who lived in our building. A man named Wade Simms. At first I thought she had married him so we wouldn't have to stay on welfare, but I was wrong. She loved him. Buddy and I came to love him too." She ran a trembling hand over her face. "After Buddy died, Mama got worse, weaker. I realize now that there was nothing wrong with her physically, but she stayed in bed most of the time. I was so scared she was going to die like Buddy had. She depended on me and Wade for everything."

She shook her head violently. "That's enough. The rest doesn't matter. It's all in the past."

"It matters if it's hurting you," he said, forcing a casual tone. "It's not in the past if you're still carrying the pain now. You said you'd share with me."

She nodded shortly, reluctantly, and let out a

slow breath. "Before long Wade started spending the night on the couch. He said Mama slept better that way."

Suddenly the truth hit Bill like a sledgehammer, and he knew what was coming next. His chest and throat hurt with the knowledge. He didn't want to hear it. He didn't want her to relive it. But he knew it was the only way she would ever be able to let it go.

"One night about two years after Buddy's death"—her voice was painfully hoarse—"he came to my room." Her slender fingers clenched in the sheets. "He said I had to be quiet or I would wake Mama. He said I couldn't upset her because she was sick. I knew he was right . . . I knew I couldn't upset her . . . and *I didn't know what to do.* I didn't know what to do."

She was shaking convulsively, and Bill had to tighten every muscle to keep from taking her in his arms. He couldn't let her stop until it was all out in the open.

"Suddenly," she whispered, "before he—before anything happened, Mama was there in the room, standing over the bed. She was screaming at me, calling me names. She was blaming me." She reached up and wiped the perspiration from her forehead with an unsteady hand. "Now, looking back, I can be rational and say that I was trapped, helpless, in a situation that was not of my making, but always in the back of my mind is the nagging feeling that there was something I could have done to keep it from happening. When Wade followed Mama to try to calm her down, I climbed out the window and left. I hid in an alley all night. The next morning I stood across the street watching as they brought Mama out on a stretcher." The words were barely audible now. "One of the neighbors told me she had accidentally taken too many sleeping pills."

He moved swiftly, urgently, and gathered her into his arms, wrapping himself around her tightly. "Don't, baby," he whispered. "Don't cry. Please don't cry."

But she wasn't. It was Bill who cried as he held her, rocking her back and forth.

After a while he thought she had gone to sleep, but when he drew back to look at her, her eyes were wide open. He cleared his throat and ran a shaky hand over his face. "What did you do after—afterward? Where did you go?"

She shrugged stiffly, as though it hurt to move. "I couldn't go to the authorities because they would have turned me over to Wade, to my stepfather." She drew in a deep, ragged breath. "So I was on my own. I found a deserted warehouse where other runaways were living, and I made a couple of friends. One of them, Sissy Keller, got papers for me so that I could go to school and get free meals. Breakfast and lunch. That was enough to keep me alive. On the weekends I worked when I could and stole when I couldn't." She shook her head. "I haven't thought of Sissy in years. One day she was simply gone. But by then I had gotten used to being alone."

Bill could feel her loosening up slightly. She was now reliving a time in which she had had more control over her life.

"I was always scared," she said. "But I got strong and I survived. I swore that someday I wouldn't have to worry about where my next meal was coming from. I wouldn't have to worry about where I would sleep for the night. I swore that someday I would have real security. Then I would never have to be afraid again."

Suddenly she gave a broken laugh and turned to look at him. "I didn't give you half," she said hoarsely. "I gave you the whole damn thing."

"I wanted it all," he said, and held out his hand. "See, it's all here. I've got all the hurt and fear here in my hand. I'll hold on to it." He clenched his fingers into a tight fist. "I'll hold it tight, and I won't ever let it get to you again. That's a promise, Lila."

Delilah pressed her face to his chest, letting his warmth ease into her flesh, absorbing the good, clean feel of him. And just for a moment she allowed herself to believe him.

Suddenly frightened, she reached up to touch his face. "You understand, don't you, Bill? You see now why I can't love," she whispered urgently. "Why I can't ever love again. I don't have any love left. I had it all burned out of me a long, long time ago."

"Don't worry about it," he said, moving his head to kiss the palm of her hand. "No one is going to force you to do anything, ever. You don't have to love me if it scares you so much. Just let me love you. You can do that." He grinned. "It's as easy as falling off a log."

Maybe, she thought, letting the hope build in her. Maybe she could do that.

Nine

"*I love you, Lila,*" the young ghost said. "*Do you love me back?*"

Delilah whimpered softly.

"I love you, Lila."

Buddy's voice was gone, replaced by another one, older and stronger. In a semi-conscious state, Delilah frowned. This wasn't the way the dream was supposed to happen.

"Wake up, baby. I love you, and I'm still holding it all in my hand. Wake up and see."

Bill.

"Bill." She said it aloud this time, smiling as she snuggled closer to him.

"Are you ever going to open your eyes?" His voice sounded wistful.

"Maybe, maybe not," she murmured. "Make it worth my while."

There was a long silence, then he said, "The avocados are only a little bit mushy."

"Nope." She shook her head, her eyes still closed. "Tempting but not good enough."

Silence again, then, "There's a muscle on the top of my foot that I can make twitch anytime I want to."

She laughed. "Is there no end to your talents? I'll check out the twitch later, when my eyes are already open."

She heard him inhale slowly. "Okay," he said, "I didn't want to do this, but you asked for it. I'm forced to bring out the big guns." He paused. "Are you ready?"

She braced herself with exaggerated movements, gripping the side of the bed with one hand, then said, "Ready."

"If you open your eyes," he said slowly, "you can see the massive physiological restructuring of the human male anatomy when brought into intimate contact with a certain desirable female of the species, hereinafter referred to as the aforementioned male's sweet patootie."

"Massive, you say?"

"At least," he said modestly.

"Okay, I'll look."

Before she could get her eyes even halfway open, he landed on top of her, knocking the breath out of her, and they rolled, arms wrapped around each other, as they shook with laughter.

Bill dropped his head to the pillow, closing his eyes, a look of satisfaction on his face. "Five days. Can you believe we've known each other for only five days?" He opened his eyes and shook his head. "It's impossible. Didn't I see you there when I got my first Boy Scout badge? Weren't you there when Joe Mack and I stole Irene Gordon's padded bra from the girls' gym and put it in Snot-Nose Sidney's locker? I swear I remember you being there." He brought her hand to his lips, kissing the palm. "I remember you, love."

"It must have been some other gorgeous blonde," she said, trying to hide the fact that she had a lump in her throat. "If I had been there, I would definitely remember. Did you get the badge for stealing the bra?" Suddenly she frowned. "Did you say five days? What day is this?"

"Friday, the most wonderful day of my life."

"The conference is . . . the conference starts today." She grabbed his wrist, turning it to look at his watch. "Oh, my gosh, we've got less than an *hour*." She threw aside the cover and scrambled from the bed. "And you—Bill, you've got to speak at the opening ceremonies!"

"That's right," he said, stretching lazily.

She ran around, grabbing up her clothes from the floor, the chair, and the nightstand. "Bill, get up."

"Mmmmm."

She dropped to her hands and knees, peering under the bed for her underwear. *"Bill, get up."*

When he simply rolled over and sent her a beatific smile, she stood up and yanked the cover off him. "Get—" She broke off as the sight of his naked body caused her to forget what she had intended to say. Lord, he had a gorgeous body.

He made a growling sound deep in his throat. "Do you know what that hungry look of yours does to me?"

He lunged at her, missing her by inches as she backed away, laughing. "We haven't got time. I can be late, but you can't. When they introduce you, someone is bound to notice that you're not there."

She stepped into her panties and was putting her arms through the straps of her bra when he dropped to his knees behind her and, with his hands on her thighs, began kissing her.

"What are you doing back there?" she said, peering over her shoulder.

"What do you think? I'm making love to the small of your back, of course."

"Of course," she said, laughing as she turned around.

"Okay, so I'll make love to your navel instead," he said, and proceeded to do exactly that.

Delilah wrapped her arms around him, closing her eyes as she pressed his face to her stomach. After a moment she shook her head. "This has to stop—immediately."

Leaning down, she kissed the top of his head, then pulled away. "Hurry . . . go take your shower. We can finish this after your speech."

"Promise?" he asked, looking back at her as he stood in the doorway leading to the bathroom.

"Promise. Now go."

She quickly pulled on the rest of her clothes

and ran a comb through her hair. She had her hand on the doorknob to leave when she suddenly turned and walked into the bathroom. Opening the curtain just a little, she said, "Kiss?"

As he soaped his chest he raised one brow and countered her question with one of his own. The single word made her gasp and laugh at the same time.

"Just a kiss this time," she said.

The kiss was wet and so was Delilah before it was over. Then, her breathing slightly labored, she ran her hand over his slick buttocks one last time and said, "I'll meet you here in a couple of hours," before reluctantly leaving him.

When she opened the door to the group's suite, she was greeted by the entire menagerie yelling in tandem, "You're late!"

"No shucks, Sherlock," she mumbled.

"You're also wet," Jack said, eyeing her damp blouse. "Is it raining in the hall?"

"Addie, get my ivory suit out of the closet," Delilah said, ignoring Jack. "Glory, underwear to match in the top drawer of the bureau. Mr. Moto, if you can find the shoes . . . they may still be in my suitcase."

As she talked she moved toward the bedroom, stripping off the clothes she had only just put on. By the time she was down to her underwear, she had reached the bathroom door.

"Booger," she said, opening the door, "you can—"

"I could soap your back for you," he offered.

"And I could soap your tongue for you." Addie's muffled but emphatic words came from inside the closet.

"The noose is growing tighter and tighter," Jack said.

Booger grinned. "Ain't it the truth." But he didn't look as though he minded at all.

"Booger, you can find my makeup case," Delilah said as she closed the bathroom door in his face.

Seconds later Delilah stepped into the steaming shower. Bill was probably through with his by now. She wished she could have shared it with him. Later, she told herself, smiling.

Delilah heard the bathroom door open, then Glory said, "Dee, I'm putting your underwear and makeup case here by the sink."

"Thanks, Glory."

"Addie sent Jack and Booger on down to save seats for us." Glory paused. "I take it you like Dr. Shelley. Do you think he'll do?"

Delilah closed her eyes, feeling the melting sweetness she always felt when she thought of him. "Bill," she said softly, then louder, "Yes, I think Dr. Shelley might work. He might be just exactly what I was looking for."

Bill had told her not to think about tomorrow, but Delilah couldn't help it. She knew from their talks that he was a general practitioner, which meant there wouldn't be fabulous wealth the way she had planned. But Delilah could adjust. With both their practices there would be security. She could put all those years of poverty and desperation behind her. And she would have Bill.

After last night he understood that she couldn't give him love, but he seemed to accept it.

Pushing the hair off her forehead, she frowned. Why did that suddenly seem wrong? Why did it suddenly feel like cheating?

She lifted her face to the water, deciding she would put off worrying about it until later. She would think about this, and all the other things she had been putting off, later. Much later.

The ballroom of the Wimberley was packed with folding chairs and people when the three women walked in. From a seat near the back, Booger whistled loudly, waving both his arms to attract their attention.

The opening ceremonies began almost as soon as they sat down, progressing at a predictably slow rate. Delilah listened for a while, then found her thoughts drifting back to the night before, the night spent in Bill's arms. She remembered how he had held her, how he had still wanted her to believe in magic. Maybe now she did. She believed in the magic of his arms around her.

She could still hear his voice in her head, the things he had whispered to her in the darkness. The secret things. The comforting things. Bill had said he would carry all her pain himself. Bill had cried for her.

Where had he come from, this man who had willingly fought the giants of her past? This man who seemed to be made of nothing but love? And how could she ever, even in her wildest fantasies, have dreamed that someone like Bill might want someone like Lila?

Shifting restlessly, she felt the worries and the doubts began to ease into her mind, slowly at first, then with a debilitating rush.

It was all too wonderful, too perfect. As Glory had said, eventually there had to be a payback.

Suddenly Addie poked her in the arm and grimaced. Then Glory leaned across Addie and whispered, "I'm sorry, Dee. We really thought he was right. I guess we should have asked more questions."

Delilah glanced at them in growing confusion. Frowning, she joined in the applause that erupted when Bill walked up to the podium. What had been in his introduction to cause them to react in such a peculiar way?

At the front of the room Bill, looking unbelievably relaxed, waited for the applause to die away, then smiled. "Dr. Wygant has told you a little about my clinic, how I got it started, and the kind of people I treat. Now he's asked me to fill you in on some of the day-to-day problems I run into in working with these people, people whose income is at or below poverty level. I could tell you how much money the average person manages to live on, but you probably wouldn't believe me. I could describe to you the condition of their homes, but trust me, you don't want to know. I could tell you the condition of their bodies when I see them for treatment, but most doctors see mistreated bodies on a regular basis so there wouldn't be anything new in that. So instead of talking about my patients, I'm going to tell you about me. I'm going to tell you why I choose to run a free clinic in a part of town that no one goes into unless they're forced to . . . or unless they happen to live there."

He paused and took a sip of water, then turned again to the audience, still at ease. "There are rewards," he said, "but the rewards are not monetary, and sometimes the rewards are so well hidden that you have to dig to find them. The fact is you pay a price for the privilege of treating these people. The work is damn hard, and on top of that, every single day you have to share their pain. Sooner or later it gets to you. There are times you hate where you are and you even hate your patients a little. You want to get away from so much mental and physical suffering. Some of these people have nothing left; they've reached the bottom. All you can do is keep their bodies going for one more day.

"But there are others who are still hanging on. Although they've lost all dignity, they've managed somehow to hold on to hope and pride. The pride makes them resent free treatment and the doctor who's offering it. Hope rests with their children. They have dreams that their children will have a better life. So when the depression gets to you, you remember the children. You want to make a difference for the children.

"In a city as modern as Houston, so many people don't know what a proper diet is. They don't know the symptoms of malnutrition or lead poisoning or mental retardation. And sometimes you find yourself confronting diseases you were certain had been wiped out in the Middle Ages. So you not only patch them up and send them on to specialists, you teach them how to keep their children healthy."

He moved his gaze slowly over the crowd. "My clinic is small and underfunded and sometimes I wonder why I'm beating my head against a brick wall. Then I see a child—just one child—whose life has been changed. And I think maybe that child won't grow up to become an adult without dignity . . . without pride . . . without hope."

After taking another sip of water, Bill began to talk about the problems of funding. He talked about government cutbacks and how he used his spare time talking to civic organizations and corporations and private citizens, anyone who might contribute to the clinic. Then he began to talk about the desperate need for qualified doctors. He didn't ask the members of the audience to give up their practices as he had. He merely told them that if anyone who was interested could give just a few hours a month, it would make a difference.

And as he spoke, as his gentle, loving voice reached out and touched the people around her, Delilah sat as still as a stone statue. She could feel Addie and Glory watching her, but she couldn't turn her head to look at them. Then suddenly she rose to her feet and walked out of the hall.

In the suite Delilah packed her bags with automatic movements. She had turned off her brain. She had turned off her emotions.

By the time her friends reached the suite, Delilah had the telephone in her hand and was checking with the airport to see when the next flight to Texas was leaving.

Her four friends quietly filed into the sitting room. Jack looked worried. Addie, after a moment of examining Delilah's face, had tears in her eyes. Booger kept his arm around Addie, comforting her for the unexplainable tears as he studied Delilah.

"He wasn't just another candidate, was he?" Glory asked quietly.

"He's such a wonderful man," Addie burst out. "That speech—" She broke off and cleared her throat.

"I have to admit it choked me up too," Booger said. "I really admire him."

Delilah closed her eyes. "You've just stated the problem." She opened her eyes. "Good Lord, think about it. Can any of you really picture me with a man like that? Jack? Booger? Come on, somebody tell me I'm the kind of woman he needs. Tell me you can see me at his side doing all those *good* things."

They all looked uncomfortable, which was the only answer Delilah had expected.

Then Glory said, "I can."

Delilah met her eyes. "You're lying. You're my friend and you want to believe I could make it with a man like Bill, but in your heart you know I'm all wrong for him."

"You can be anything you want to be, Dee," Glory said urgently. "And Bill doesn't seem to think you're the wrong woman for him."

Delilah sighed. "Bill hasn't looked into the future and seen what I've seen." She paused, staring down at her hands. "I've never told any of you about my life before I joined the rest of you. Those people . . . those people he helps, I was one of them. It was bad enough when my family was alive. Then I was alone, and it was even worse."

Lifting her chin in determination, she said, "There are only two things in life that scare me. One is poverty. You all heard what he said down there. He's chosen to live in poverty. He's free to do that. And I'm free to choose not to." She shook her head and whispered, "I can't go back to that. I can't see it all around me and not relive every second of it."

Silence fell heavily over them, then suddenly Booger said, "And the other thing?"

Everyone turned to stare at him. "What?" Delilah asked, frowning in confusion.

"You said there were two things that scare you," he said, his voice as calm and objective as always. "One is poverty. What's the other?"

Without realizing it, Booger had hit upon the key to why she had panicked, why she knew she had to leave. Closing her eyes, Delilah felt once more the emotions that had swept through her when she had listened to Bill's speech. She had

had a tremendous, glowing surge of pride. And with it had come the treasonous thought that financial security didn't matter. She wanted Bill anyway.

What she had felt for Bill at that moment came very close to love. And that scared the hell out of her.

She opened her eyes and looked at Booger. "Love," she said hoarsely. "Love and poverty."

"And with Bill you would have both," Glory said, looking tired and sad. Sad for Delilah.

Delilah shook her head wildly. She wanted to deny it. She wanted to scream that she didn't love him. She couldn't possibly love him. But the words wouldn't come.

When they heard a knock on the door, Delilah knew who was there, but she didn't move. She stood by the window, looking at the bay as Addie opened the door.

"Hi, Addie," Bill said. "Lila was supposed to meet me in my room. Have you—"

He broke off and walked into the room, stopping short when he saw Delilah's bags. "Lila?"

After a moment of tense silence the group began moving out of the suite, then the door closed softly behind them.

Bill walked closer to where Delilah stood and said again, "Lila?"

This time she could hear the fear in his voice. She couldn't let it get to her. She had to pull this off. For him. For her.

Standing up straighter, she smiled slightly. "I

didn't ever tell you why I came to Acapulco early, did I? I came to see the group, of course, but I also came to find a husband," she said, keeping her voice calm and steady. "The group decided to help by having a scavenger hunt to find a rich doctor for me." She met his eyes. "You were my rich doctor, Bill. Don't you see how funny that is?" Her voice broke on the last word, and she paused to regain control. "Why didn't you tell me? You mentioned working in the slums, but I thought it was the pro bono work that we all do. Why didn't you tell me about the clinic?"

He ran an unsteady hand through his hair. "I don't know," he murmured, shaking his head. "I guess I didn't think it was important. There was so much more we had to talk about."

"You didn't think it was important?" Her voice was angry and incredulous. "When you knew how I felt about being poor?"

"I didn't know. You never said— You said you wanted to be secure."

"What in hell do you think security is?" she asked, her eyes wide and angry.

A strange smile twitched across his lips, then died. "Not money," he said softly. "Not to me."

"It is to me," she said, forcing the words through tight lips. "It is to me."

There was no expression on his face now, but something told Delilah he was staying upright by sheer force of will. She drew in several deep breaths, fighting her need to hold him.

She swung away from him abruptly. "Will you stop looking at me with those damned stray-dog eyes?" she told him. "Just leave, Bill. You're a nice man. Find yourself a nice woman. One with no hangups, no horrors from the past for you to deal with. Find someone who can give you what you need, because I can't."

"You have me a little confused." His voice sounded strange, different. "Are you leaving because I don't make a lot of money or because I'm nice? Which is it, Lila?"

"It's— What difference— It's both," she got out finally. "You're too nice and too—"

"*Nice*," he said, spitting the word at her as he moved between her and the window, forcing her to look at him. "You keep saying that."

Suddenly his face changed, growing ugly with fury. He grabbed her roughly by the shoulders and moved her backward until she bumped into the couch, then he pressed her down with his body. "Would you stay with me if I were not so nice?" he asked, his voice harsh. "If that's what it takes, then to hell with nice."

He kissed her then. And for Delilah it was like walking through hell. There was no love in the kiss. There wasn't even passion. The grinding strength of his anger didn't hurt her, but the absence of his love broke her heart.

"Is this better, Delilah?" he said in a raspy voice. "Not quite so nice? Will you stay with me now?"

He stared down at her. Delilah didn't know what he saw in her face, but after a moment he closed his eyes tightly and pushed away from her. Rising to his feet, he turned and walked a few steps away, his shoulders sagging as though he were suddenly very weary.

With his back to her he said, "You've been engaged to half a dozen wealthy men. If money was all you needed, why didn't one of them work out? Why, Lila? I'll tell you why. Because you were looking for more. You needed more. And whether you admit it or not, you found what you needed with me. Two hours ago . . . two hours ago—" He broke off and inhaled slowly. "Now suddenly you're scared. But I don't think it's poverty that frightens you. I think you're afraid of being helpless. And that's also why you won't let yourself love."

He walked over to where she still sat on the couch and knelt beside her. "Someday, babe, you're going to figure out that the lack of money doesn't make you helpless unless you let it . . . and neither does love."

Delilah heard the words, but she couldn't take in their meaning. She was too confused. Too afraid. She was running for her life and couldn't think of anything except getting away from the pain. From Bill.

"You're hurting, Lila," he whispered softly. "I wish I could make it all better. But this time I can't. You have to work through this by yourself." He drew in a rough breath. "When you do, I'll be—"

"Don't say it," she begged in desperation. "Don't wait for me, Bill. This is the end. It was a beauti-

ful dream, but I'm a realist. Dreams fade," she said. "Reality is always there."

He stared at her for a moment, then his mouth twitched violently. "Yes, I guess you're right," he said wearily. "Reality doesn't go away."

He rose to his feet and walked to the door. When he had opened it he said, without turning to look at her, "Good-bye, Lila."

Then he walked out of the room.

Ten

Delilah turned slightly, studying the face of the man in the driver's seat of the Mercedes.

Dr. Michael Linden was tall, blond, and had a smile that could charm a Dallas Cowboy linebacker. His clothes were tailor-made, discreetly elegant, tasteful, and expensive. His hair had been cut by the best stylist in the area, and there wasn't a single lock out of place. On his wrist he wore a simple gold watch, and on his middle finger of his left hand, a simple sapphire ring. His reputation as a plastic surgeon had brought his patients from both coasts and even from Europe. He was intelligent and entertaining. Dr. Michael Linden was perfect.

She glanced away from him, staring at the street ahead. Yes, she thought without emotion, he was perfect.

It had been four months since Acapulco. Only four months, but so much had happened in those months. Booger and Addie had set their wedding date, and the group was planning to fly to Kansas on the night before and celebrate by having what Booger called a Madness Marathon.

Jack had called Delilah several times in the last few months, talking for hours, building his courage to make a career move. She never gave him advice. She merely let him get all the worries out in the open. Someone had done that for her once, and she knew what a cleansing experience it could be.

The last time she talked to Jack had been in the days immediately after he had flown to Cincinnati to tell his parents about his decision to give up surgery. It had been, as expected, a rough experience for him. His father had been angry, his mother sympathetic but confused. But Jack had taken the first step, and Delilah was proud of him.

As for Glory and Alan, Delilah saw them often. Delilah had tried on more than one occasion to apologize personally to Alan for the pain she had caused him in Acapulco, but Alan refused to recognize any need for apology.

Glory was still saddened by her inability to have children, but at least now she was able to talk openly about it. Glory had been an only child and had looked forward to raising a large family. Although she still wasn't ready to think about adopting, Delilah was positive it was only a matter of time.

And what about the last member of the group,

she asked herself silently. What had Delilah Jones accomplished in the past four months?

Four months, she repeated silently. Eternity.

Inhaling slowly, she pulled her attention back to the man beside her. Moments later Michael was in the process of recounting the events of a recent trip to Switzerland when the music on the radio faded and was replaced by the soft voice of the KOAC announcer.

It didn't surprise Delilah that Michael listened to that particular station. The peppy chatter of the upwardly mobile stations or the harsh openness of the rock stations would have disrupted the calm atmosphere that surrounded Michael. And nothing was allowed to do that.

On station KOAC even the newscaster spoke in soft, reassuring tones, making the corruption, crime, and catastrophes reported seem remote and therefore less disturbing.

Suddenly, as the soothing tones of the newscaster began to actually form words and penetrate her consciousness, Delilah caught her breath, then reached over quickly to turn up the volume.

". . . only minor damages and no reported deaths in Acapulco; however, isolated areas in the nearby mountains, closer to the epicenter of the earthquake, were reported to have experienced widespread destruction and loss of life. The earthquake registered 7.3 on the Richter scale. In Acapulco residents are preparing for the aftershocks which could cause even more extensive damage. The military—"

"Turn right at the next corner." Delilah said abruptly.

"I beg your pardon."

"Turn right at the next corner. I'm sorry, Michael, but this is an emergency."

She had to talk to Glory. She had to see if her friend had heard anything about Nuevo Oviedo. Delilah gave Michael brief but complete directions, and fifteen minutes later, when the car stopped in front of Glory's house, Delilah jumped out.

"I'll take a cab home, Michael," she said as she was closing the door of the Mercedes.

"But, Delilah—"

Delilah didn't hear the rest. Mrs. Anderson, Glory's housekeeper, opened the front door for her, and as Delilah opened her mouth to ask for Glory, Alan walked into the entry hall.

"Glory is on the phone with Jack," he said before she had a chance to ask. "And she's already talked to the Mexican authorities."

Delilah followed him into the study, then straightened her back in an automatic reaction to the grim look on Glory's face.

"Yes, that's right . . . tomorrow. Just a second, Jack. Dee just walked in." She turned to Delilah. "I suppose you've heard?"

Delilah shook her head. "Only that a quake had hit near Acapulco. They didn't say anything about Nuevo Oviedo."

Glory bit her lip. "I'm afraid it's bad. The village was almost at the center. Equipment and a few doctors have already been flown in, but we're going too. Booger and Addie are already on their way from Kansas, and Jack is flying in early tomorrow morning."

When Delilah nodded, Glory turned back to the telephone to talk to Jack.

Alan moved toward the door. "If we're leaving tomorrow," he said, "I'd better start making arrangements."

"You're going too?"

He turned slightly, gazing at his wife. "It's going to be painful for her, maybe even dangerous. I won't ask her not to go, but if anything happens, I'll be there."

Delilah nodded, then sat on the leather couch to wait for Glory. As soon as Glory hung up the phone, she walked over and sat down beside Delilah.

"I don't think I've quite taken it in yet," Glory said. "All those children in the marketplace . . . that beautiful little girl who gave me her cornhusk doll—" She met Delilah's eyes. "Dee, she could be hurt . . . or worse." She shuddered, then glanced at Delilah's long satin dress. "Why are you here? I tried to get you on the phone earlier, then I remembered you had a date with Michael. Where is he?"

"I had him drop me off here when I heard the report on the radio."

Glory studied Delilah's face. "I don't suppose I even have to ask if you're going with us?"

For months Delilah had held many pictures in her mind. One picture was a large house, a welcoming family, an autocratic old man, and laughing children. The Fuentes household.

"No," she said quietly, "you don't have to ask."

Because the mountain road had been blocked by a series of rock slides, the group was flown to Nuevo Oviedo by helicopter. Delilah began treating victims the minute she and the others set their feet on the ground. She worked frantically alongside doctors of all nationalities, caring men and women who hadn't hesitated in responding to the village's need.

The beautiful little village of Nuevo Oviedo had changed beyond recognition. The church, which had sustained minor damages, was the only building left standing on the plaza. The others had been destroyed or irreparably damaged. By some miracle the little garden in the center had been left untouched, its beauty incongruous somehow, like a butterfly fluttering over a battlefield.

Even though the possibility of further aftershocks was a serious one, the church was considered safe and had been turned into a temporary hospital. It was there, on the afternoon of her arrival, that Delilah ran into Arturo Fuentes. With quiet dignity he told her of the death of his grandfather, Tomás Fuentes, the old man who had made himself responsible for the welfare of Nuevo Oviedo.

Like most of the village, the Fuentes house and its occupants had survived the initial quake, but later the old man had gone out to search for Jaime, the seven-year-old with the dirty face and bright eyes who had wandered away from the yard. Señor Fuentes had been looking in the forest, near the valley of rainbows, when the first aftershock brought a tree down on him. Jaime was still missing.

Delilah accepted the news without flinching. She knew that someday the shock and anger and pain she was holding in would hit her hard, but she couldn't allow herself to think of the quiet, dignified old man or the laughing little boy. She didn't have time for emotion. There were too many people who needed her.

In the church the wooden pews had been removed, and the floor was lined with wall-to-wall pallets and salvaged mattresses. Doctors worked on their knees beside the patients—men, women, and children all lying side by side, like a scene from a Civil War movie.

Delilah was stooped beside a little girl with a gaping cut on her leg when she glanced up and saw Bill beside her. He had his back to her as he held a stethoscope to the abdomen of a woman in the advanced stages of pregnancy.

After a moment and without pausing in his work, he said, "A copter just arrived with more supplies, so we don't have to keep rationing the Novocain."

There was no stiffness in his voice, no awkwardness in the air between them. His tone was casual, as though it had been four minutes since they had last been together rather than four months.

Delilah nodded, then smoothed the air from her patient's forehead and said, "Bill, she's frightened. Could you tell her how I'll go about cleaning and stitching the cut? I don't want to make it worse for her."

As he checked a burn on his own patient's shoulder, Bill spoke softly, occasionally turning his head to smile at the little girl in Delilah's care. After a while the girl began to relax. She even returned Bill's smile.

The girl's reaction came as no surprise to Delilah. She knew exactly what effect Bill had on the female of the species, in fact, on anyone who came in contact with him.

When he had finished with his patient, Bill got to his feet and looked around, checking to see where he was needed next. Before he could walk away, Delilah rose to stand beside him.

"Bill, I heard about Jaime and Señor Fuentes. I'm sorry," she said quietly, meeting his gaze. "What will happen to the village without him? How can they possibly recover from this without his help?"

"Arturo will take over," he said. "He's young and determined. Although I don't think he realizes it yet, *Abuelo*'s dreams have become his dreams." He paused, drawing in a deep breath. "I can't seem to get it through my head that he's gone. I can't believe that he'll never be here again."

Delilah had taken a step toward him when two

more patients were carried into the makeshift hospital. With efficient movements Bill began to examine the worst of them before the volunteers could even get the man to a bed.

When Delilah saw that Booger was handling the other newcomer, she turned away and began checking the progress of those who had already received treatment. There was no time to think. No time to feel.

At dusk on the first day there was suddenly a lull in the work. Everyone had a chance to catch their breath while they waited for the volunteers to clear away more debris and locate more victims.

Bill knew he should be using the hiatus to rest, but he was too keyed up to sleep. He sat on the grass under a tree in the little garden in the center of the square.

When he closed his eyes he saw her face, as always. She looked thinner now. The fine bones of her cheeks were more sharply defined. Now, instead of strikingly beautiful, she was hauntingly beautiful. Appropriate somehow for a woman who had been haunting him for months.

When she had seen him kneeling beside her in the church, there had been no discernible expression on her face. Although he had looked deeply into her eyes, he had found nothing there. It was as though a light had gone out. The passionate heart was missing, and its absence left a chill in the air.

Bill couldn't count the number of nights he had stayed awake worrying about her, afraid for her, wondering if she was still having the nightmare that was so painful for her.

Over and over again in his mind he had heard her say, "It was a beautiful dream, but I'm a realist. Dreams fade. Reality is always there."

Whose reality, he wondered. His reality was apparently worlds apart from hers, because not one memory, not one infinitesimal part of what he felt for her had faded. Delilah hadn't left his thoughts for a single moment in the months they had been apart. When he wasn't actively thinking of her, he could feel her, all around him, inside him.

This was his reality, and Bill had no doubt that it would last forever. She was a part of him now. Sometimes he hated her for that. Sometimes when her frustratingly nebulous presence made his heart beat fast and his palms sweat, he cursed her. She had left him with the taste of her still in his mouth, the feel of her still on his fingers, the fire of her still in his loins. She had left him with the knowledge that he would forever have the echoes of the woman, but never the woman herself.

Like Nuevo Oviedo, he had somehow survived the earthquake that was Lila, but the aftershocks threatened to destroy him.

A few minutes later Delilah's friends arrived in a group and collapsed on the grass close around Bill, each one dirty and exhausted.

Bill had noticed Glory's husband working beside the other nonmedical volunteers as they searched through the ruins for survivors, and had wondered about his presence here. He had read newspaper articles about Alan and knew he was a rich and powerful man. He didn't look it now. He looked like a tired man watching carefully over his tired wife. He looked like the kind of man Bill wanted to know.

Jack lay on his back with his eyes closed, but after a moment he murmured, "I'm not really this tired . . . it's an illusion. And I'm not really hungry. Why didn't someone think to stop by the food tent?"

"I'm too tired to eat," Glory said, then glanced at Booger, who was lying with his head in Addie's lap. "Speaking of food, have you lost weight?"

"The thought of getting married would scare the appetite out of anyone, even the Bountiful Beast here," Jack said.

Without moving, without opening his eyes, Booger said, "Addie is making me eat healthy stuff. I haven't had a Twinkie or burrito in months."

"Good for Addie," Glory said, snuggling closer to her husband. "I worried about how much weight you had put on since Dallas."

"I happen to have big bones," Booger said.

Jack opened one eye to look at Booger. "Dinosaurs don't have bones that big."

"Leave him alone or I'll give you a fat lip," Addie said. Her voice was tired and without noticeable emphasis.

Booger turned to kiss her stomach. "My hero."

She grinned down at him, then glanced around at the group. "You'll all have to accept the fact that Boog's changing and growing. Inside instead of outside. He even surprises me sometimes. I never dreamed he could be so romantic—stop laughing! He really is. He recites the most beautiful poetry to me."

The group reacted with raucous laughter. Even Bill had to smile at the thought of Booger reciting poetry.

Alan, with a perfectly straight face, said, "I'm sure it's . . . very moving."

"Nothing but the best for my Addie." Booger picked up her hand and stared up into her eyes.

Bill realized that the large, innocent-faced man they all called Booger had somehow managed to make his friends relax. He shook his head. Delilah's friends were an extraordinary group of people.

Glancing up, he found himself the center of attention and knew then why they had chosen this spot to rest.

"How has she been?" he asked quietly.

The others turned to look at Glory, who shrugged slightly. "Alan and I see her more often than we used to, but I just don't know, Bill. She dates quite a bit and still seems to be looking for her successful doctor, but something is different. She won't talk about Acapulco, and she won't let me talk about it either."

Glory shifted restlessly. "She doesn't realize I know this, but I've heard gossip at the hospital and the word is out that Dee's spending an awful lot of her time working at a free clinic." She shook her head. "I'm afraid she's as hard to read as ever."

Addie frowned. "I've always thought of Dee as being totally independent, but something in her eyes—"

Booger sat up. "Loneliness," he said. "It wasn't there before. But I noticed it the minute I saw her this time."

Jack nodded. "Yes, loneliness, but that's not all. Delilah has always distanced herself from people, from emotions. On the surface she seems even more distant, but I have a feeling it's a snow job. I think she's actively participating in life now." He met Bill's eyes. "In a way, I kind of hate to see it. It seems painful for her."

"I'll tell you something really strange," Alan said. "On the plane from Dallas I looked at the list of doctors and told Delilah that you would be here too. I figured she would be shocked or embarrassed . . . something. The funny thing is, she didn't show even a hint of surprise. There was no reaction at all."

Bill leaned his head back against the tree, smiling a tiny, crooked smile. "No," he said softly, "she wouldn't have shown surprise. Lila knew I would be here."

The next few days were among the roughest of Delilah's life. Just when she would let herself believe that they were winning the battle, someone would be uncovered in the rubble or a group would come down from isolated places in the mountains seeking help.

It never let up. She would catch a few minutes of uneasy sleep at a time, then get up and go back to work. Delilah had turned off all feeling four months earlier, but in the brief periods that she managed to sleep, her emotions caught up with her. Her dreams were full of frightened children, *Abuelo*'s carved-granite face, and Bill's pain-filled eyes. After a while she simply refused to go to sleep during her rest breaks.

Then, five days after they had arrived, activity in the church began to slow down, and eventually it stopped altogether. The people who had sustained life-threatening injuries had been taken out by helicopter, and the ones with less serious problems had been patched up and were waiting now for the road to be cleared so they could be moved to hospitals in Mexico City and Acapulco.

It was mid-morning of the sixth day when Delilah made her way through what had once been Nuevo Oviedo's marketplace. She remembered the afternoon she had walked through this street with Bill. They had returned after siesta time, and he had bought the red belt for her.

She kept the belt in a satin-lined box in a drawer under her lingerie.

Other memories began to demand attention, trying to push into her mind—glimpses of the Fuentes family, the cliff overlooking the valley of rainbows, patchwork eyes looking at her with so much love. But Delilah wouldn't let the memories in. She couldn't let them in.

For several seconds something other than memories had been hovering on the edge of her consciousness, and finally it penetrated. A faint, high-pitched sound came from a wooden building behind the market stands.

She frowned, moving nearer. The quake had hit at night. No one should have been here. The volunteers hadn't even bothered to search in this part of the village. They were concentrating on private homes.

When she heard the noise again, she bent and began to pull away planks and pieces of metal.

"What is it?" Bill asked, coming out of nowhere to stand beside her. "Did you hear something?"

She nodded. "I think so . . . I don't know, maybe it was an animal . . . a kitten."

They both stood very still and listened. The sound came again. This time it was clearer. And it wasn't an animal. It was a soft, whimpering sound, the kind only a suffering human can make.

Delilah dropped to her knees and began to pull at the rubble.

"Wait," Bill said sharply. Then he began to speak loudly and clearly in Spanish. Occasionally he would pause to listen for a response.

At last, as though the words came from a great distance, they heard, *"Jaime, Guillermo . . . estoy Jaime."*

Delilah felt her heart jerk in her chest. Jaime. The missing child. The bright young boy who had tried to teach her Spanish. They had to get him out. They couldn't let anything happen to the child *Abuelo* had died trying to find.

Together they began to move the rubble out of the way, working silently, frantically. The material was lightweight, and soon they had cleared a tunnel of sorts. Bill spoke regularly to the boy, and Delilah knew he was testing the child's reactions, trying to gauge how extensive his injuries were.

Judging by the nearness of Jaime's voice, they seemed to be only a few feet away from him when they came upon a solid stone structure, an oven or furnace of some sort.

Bill sat back on his heels and studied it. "I don't think we're going to be able to get past this," he said. He glanced back at her. "Lila, you'd better find Arturo. He'll get some workers to help us."

She stared into his eyes, silent as the dust settled around them. It was only a second, a tiny piece of time, but it seemed to last forever. Then she nodded. "I'll be back as soon as I can," she said, and turned to crawl out of the tunnel.

She hadn't realized they had dug so deeply inside the building, but they must have, because it felt as though hours had passed before she finally stood up outside the building.

The market street was long and straight, but it was filled with remnants of the wooden stalls. She moved as quickly as possible and had gone perhaps a hundred yards when she ran, literally, into

Alan. She turned a corner and almost knocked him over in her rush to get help.

"What is it?" He frowned as he surveyed her face and torn shirt.

"We—Bill and I—" She broke off and tried to catch her breath. "We've found the missing Fuentes boy. He's trapped in a—"

Grabbing Alan's arm, she pulled him around the corner and pointed toward the collapsed building behind the marketplace. "See that building? We—"

At that moment a sound reached them. There was no giant explosion, merely a low, shifting rumble. And suddenly the pile of rubble seemed to grow smaller.

There was a bright flash in Delilah's brain, then a convulsion in her chest, and the world stopped.

Without a word to Alan she began to run back the way she had come, keeping her eyes on the place where she had left the only thing that mattered in the world as she felt her way back across the ocean of debris.

When she reached the ruins she found that the tunnel they had cleared was still there. She dropped to her hands and knees and began to crawl, unaware that Alan was behind her until she reached a place that was impassable. Earth and rock filled the tunnel.

A frantic, whimpering sound came from her throat, and she began to claw her way through, tearing at the material with bleeding fingers. She was reacting instinctively. Rational thought had no place in her mind. She knew only one thing: She had to get to Bill.

"Dee, wait," Alan said from behind her. "We've got to go get help."

"You go. Go get help," she said, her voice fierce. "But don't ask me to wait. Bill's in there somewhere."

He hesitated for only a moment, then turned and began to crawl out of the tunnel.

Moving steadily, Delilah continued to clear the same area they had cleared together minutes earlier. Her hands didn't falter, but as she worked, she prayed.

God, she begged silently, *I need help. I know when Mama died I said I didn't need You anymore. I said a lot of things I shouldn't have said. That's because I'm not a very good person. I know that. But Bill is. God, he's—he's such a good man. Please, if You'll just help him . . . just watch over him, I'll be better. I swear to You I'll try to be a better person.* She swallowed hard. *But if it's not possible . . . if Bill dies, please, God . . . let me die too.*

It seemed that hours had passed when Delilah realized she had almost reached the spot where they had had to stop because of the brick structure. Every time she moved a piece of rubble aside she expected to find Bill beneath it. But she didn't find him. She had called out to him several times. But he didn't answer.

She told herself that Bill simply hadn't heard her. The building was still settling, making creaking, shifting noises. Combined with the insulating layer of dust in the air, that was enough to obscure her voice.

She had to tell herself something. She couldn't believe he had died without her. She refused to believe it.

At last, after pulling what must have once been a small table out of the way, she reached the brick structure. And Bill wasn't there.

She felt a wave of relief sweep over her, making her weak. He must have found a way around it. That's why he hadn't heard her. He was deeper into the building than she had thought.

"Bill?" she said softly. She was afraid to shout, afraid any loud noise would cause another collapse.

Holding herself still, she listened, but she heard nothing other than the sound of settling debris.

"Bill," she said again, just a little louder.

Then faintly she heard, "I'm here, baby."

Closing her eyes, she dropped her head to her hands as she crouched in the tunnel and began to shake.

"Lila?"

She raised her head and ran her hands across her face, making muddy streaks on her fingers. "I don't know how to reach you," she said hoarsely. "Are you all right?"

"I'm okay . . . I think." His voice sounded very far away.

"This is no time to be cryptic," she said, almost angry. "What does that mean?"

Incredibly she thought she heard him laugh. "Something fell on my left hand. It's bleeding and so numb I can't really feel it, but I think it's simply bruised."

"Thank you, God," she whispered, then louder, "And Jaime?"

"He's in remarkably good condition, considering what he's been through. He's dehydrated and his left forearm may be broken. It's trapped under a metal desk."

She hesitated, then said, "Bill, Alan has gone to get some workers. They'll be able to help Jaime. Can you get out?"

"No—I don't know." He paused, then said, "I can't leave him, Lila. He's so scared."

She should have known better than to ask. He wouldn't be Bill if he could leave an injured and traumatized child.

Seconds later she heard voices in the tunnel behind her, then suddenly the place was crowded. Arturo spoke to Bill, asking his advice on what direction they should take. When they had decided, Arturo turned to Delilah.

"It will be better if you leave," he said. "I thank you for finding Jaime, but there is no need for you to put yourself in further danger."

She shook her head. "I can help. And if you don't need my help, I'll stay out of the way. But I won't leave."

He studied her face for a moment, then nodded and the work began.

Two and a half hours later, both Bill and Jaime were brought safely out of the shifting wreckage.

Later, at the church, the group stood around

joking with Bill as he sat on a wooden crate and allowed Delilah to bandage the cut on his hand.

"It's a bad cut," Delilah told him, her voice subdued, "but luckily none of the bones are broken."

He didn't respond. He merely sat looking up at her. He hadn't taken his eyes off her once since they had arrived at the church. Delilah wondered what it was he saw in her face.

When she had applied the last piece of tape, Delilah murmured, "Excuse me," then walked calmly away from the group and out of the church.

Without a word Bill stood and followed her. He found her in the plaza garden leaning against a tree, her body trembling violently.

When he pulled her into his arms, she pushed tightly against him, as though she couldn't get close enough.

"It's okay . . . it's over now," he said, stroking her hair. "You're simply having a delayed reaction to the scare. You'll be all right in a few minutes."

She pressed her face to his throat, moaning, "I think I'm going to be sick."

He moved with her to one of the stone benches and pushed her head down between her knees. "Take deep breaths, sweetheart. Slow, deep breaths."

After a moment she turned her head sideways to look up at him. "Bill, I think I'm in big trouble."

"You're pregnant?"

Delilah gave a choking laugh. He sounded intrigued by the possibility.

"Not that kind of trouble," she said. She raised herself up and folded her hands in her lap. "When

I couldn't find you . . . when I didn't know what had happened to you, I promised God I would be a good person if—" She broke off, feeling the trembling begin again in her limbs.

"If what?" he asked softly.

"'If . . . if He would just let you live," she whispered. "And He did."

"Yes, He did." He raised one thick brow. "So what's the problem?"

She lifted her gaze to his. "Bill, I don't know how to be a good person. What if I can't do it? What if I've got bitch in my bones?"

He laughed, putting his arm around her. "I know your bones intimately. There's not a bitchy one in the bunch."

She glanced away from him. "I hurt you," she said. "I will never forgive myself for that. Never."

There was a long, taut silence, then he said, "Why not? I did."

She turned back to him, studying his features. "Did you?" When he nodded she drew in a rough breath. "That's only because you're Mr. Nice Guy. You do that kind of thing."

That's only because I love you, he corrected her silently.

"Having you forgive me shouldn't be that easy," she said tightly. "You should make me go down on my hands and knees and beg your forgiveness." Her lips twisted in a bitter smile. "If I thought it would make up for some of the pain, I'd do it."

He stared at her in confusion, then rose to his

feet. "I don't understand you. Would you really do something like that?" he asked. "For me?"

There wasn't a trace of the old aloofness in her face as she met his gaze and said, "For you, Bill?" then slowly dropped to her knees beside him.

"Sweet heaven, Lila!" he exclaimed, pulling her to her feet and back into his arms.

A long time later Bill and Delilah sat on the grass under a tree. His arms were wrapped around her waist as she leaned back against his chest and filled him in on what had been happening in her life since Acapulco.

"After a couple of weeks I went back to find the warehouse that I told you about, where I had stayed for a while," she said, moving her face against his arm as she spoke. "It wasn't there. They tore it down years ago. The area is just as bad as I remembered, but I didn't run from it. I made myself talk to the people who live and work there. I began to see them as people instead of something out of a nightmare. Some of them I liked, some I didn't . . . they were just like people everywhere." She twisted her head to look up at him. "The memory of those years I spent there had grown all out of proportion in my mind. Or maybe it was simply that you brought things into perspective for me. I had convinced myself—no, I really believed—that money would bring me security. Finding a rich doctor was part of that. It was part of the dream, the image I had carried around with me for so long. We would be the perfect couple, and nothing could touch us. That image was security to me. I relied on it."

She grimaced. "It didn't take long after I left Mexico for me to realize that the only time in my life I had ever felt really secure was when I was in your arms."

"Do I get to say 'I told you so' now, or do you want me to wait until later?" he asked, dropping a kiss on her shoulder.

She laughed, then turned her head to meet his eyes. "Being without a lot of money doesn't scare me now. And I think I can be a real help at your clinic. I've never thought of myself as an altruistic sort of person, but I really believe I'll be good at it. I know how the people feel. I know what they're going through so I'll be able to communicate with them."

"I believe you," he said. "I've always believed in you . . . besides, you promised God you'd be a good person."

Her expression became wary. "Exactly how good do you think He'll expect me to be?"

He laughed. "I don't know about God, but for me, you'll do just the way you are."

She drew in a shaky breath. "I hope so, Bill. That's one of the things I haven't come to grips with yet. I know, deep in my soul, that you deserve better than me."

His arms tightened around her. "And I know, deep in my soul, that there isn't another woman on earth I want or need. There isn't another woman who could make me happy. So if I can't have you,

I'll have no one," he whispered. "Because it's you I love, Lila."

She felt her mouth go dry. Clenching her fists, she said, "I . . . Bill, I—you see, I really do—" She broke off, closing her eyes in defeat.

"That's the other thing I haven't come to grips with," she said tightly. "I want you. I need you desperately. If I lost you I would bleed to death from the heart . . . but the idea of love still terrifies me."

Bill pulled her back into his arms, holding on to her with all his strength. She could call it whatever she wanted to call it, but from where he was standing, it felt like love. It felt a lot like love.

"Don't worry about it," he said softly. "Don't even think about it. On our fiftieth wedding anniversary we'll gather all the children and grandchildren around us. We'll put the problem to them, and they can help you decide whether what you feel for me is love or not."

He framed her face with both hands, feeling his chest expand painfully at the depth of emotion in her beautiful golden eyes. For him. All for him.

"Until then," he whispered hoarsely, "I'll hold you, Lila, and I'll love you. And I'll wait."

THE EDITOR'S CORNER

I feel envious of you. I wish I could look forward to reading next month's LOVESWEPTs for the first time! How I would love to sit back on a succession of the fine spring days coming up and read these six novels. They are just great and were loads of fun for us here to work on.

Starting off not with a bang but an *explosion,* we have the first novel in *The Pearls of Sharah* trilogy, **LEAH'S STORY,** LOVESWEPT #330, by Fayrene Preston. When Zarah, an old gypsy woman, gave her the wondrous string of creamy pearls, promising that a man with cinnamon-colored hair would enter her life and magic would follow, Leah insisted she didn't believe in such pretty illusions. But when handsome Stephen Tanner appeared that night at the carnival, she saw her destiny in his dark eyes and fiery hair. He found her fascinating, beautiful, an enchantress whose gypsy lips had never known passion until the fire of his kisses made her tremble and their sweetness made her melt. Leah had never fit in anywhere but with the gypsies, and she feared Stephen would abandon her as her parents had. Could he teach her she was worthy of his love, that the magic was in her, not the mysterious pearls? Do remember that this marvelous book is also available in hardcover from Doubleday.

Unforgettable Rylan Quaid and Maggie McSwain, that fantastic couple you met in **RUMOR HAS IT,** get their own love story next month in Tami Hoag's **MAN OF HER DREAMS,** LOVESWEPT #331. When Rylan proposes to Maggie at his sister's wedding, joy and fierce disappointment war in her heart. She has loved him forever, wants him desperately. But could he really be such a clod that he would suggest it was time he settled down, and she might as well be the one he did it with? Maggie has to loosen the reins he holds on his passion, teach Ry that he has love to give—and that she is the one great love of his life. Ry figures he's going to win the darling Maggie by showing he's immune to her sizzling charms. . . . This is a love story as heartwarming as it is hot!

From first to last you'll be breathless with laughter and a tear or two as you revel in Joan Elliott Pickart's **HOLLY'S**

(continued)

HOPE, LOVESWEPT #332. Holly Chambers was so beautiful . . . but she appeared to be dead! Justin Hope, shocked at the sight of bodies lying everywhere, couldn't imagine what disaster had befallen the pretty Wisconsin town or how he could help the lovely woman lying so pale and limp on the grass. When mouth-to-mouth resuscitation turned into a kiss full of yearning and heat, Justin felt his spirits soar. He stayed in town and his relationship with Holly only crackled more and warmed more with each passing day. But he called the world his oyster, while Holly led a safe life in her little hometown. Was love powerful enough to change Justin's dreams and to transform Holly, who had stopped believing in happily-ever-after? The answer is pure delight.

Next, we have the thrilling **FIRE AND ICE,** LOVE-SWEPT #333, from the pen—oops—word processor of talented Patt Bucheister. Lauren McLean may look serene, even ice-princess reserved, but on the inside she is full of fiery passion for John Zachary, her boss, her unrequited love . . . the man who has scarcely noticed her during the two or three years she has worked for him. When John unexpectedly gains custody of his young daughter, it is Lauren to the rescue of the adorable child as well as the beleaguered (and adorable!) father. Starved for ecstasy, Lauren wants John more than her next breath . . . and he is wild about her. But she knows far too much about the pain of losing the people she's become attached to. When John melts the icy barriers that keep Lauren remote, the outpouring of passion's fire will have you turning the pages as if they might scorch your fingers.

There's real truth-in-titling in Barbara Boswell's **SIM-PLY IRRESISTIBLE,** LOVESWEPT #334, because it *is* a simply irresistibly marvelous romance. I'm sure you really won't be able to put it down. Surgeon Jason Fletcher, the hospital heartbreaker to whom Barbara has previously introduced you, is a gorgeously virile playboy with no scruples . . . until he steps in to protect Laura Novak from a hotshot young doctor. Suddenly Jason—the man who has always prided himself on not having a possessive bone in his body—feels jealous and protective of Laura. Laura's pulse races with excitement when he claims her, but when a near accident shatters her com-

(continued)

posure and forces long-buried emotions to the surface, grief and fury are transformed into wild passion. Danger lurks for Jason in Laura's surrender though, because she is the first woman he has wanted to keep close. And he grows desperate to keep his distance! Jason has always got what he wanted, but Laura has to make him admit he wishes for love.

We close out our remarkable month with one of the most poignant romances we've published, **MERMAID**, **LOVESWEPT** #335, by Judy Gill. In my judgment this story ranks right up there with Dorothy Garlock's beautiful **A LOVE FOR ALL TIME**, LOVESWEPT #6. Mark Forsythe knew it was impossible, an illusion—he'd caught a golden-haired mermaid on his fishing line! But Gillian Lockstead was deliciously real, a woman of sweet mystery who filled him with a joy he'd forgotten existed. When Gillian gazed up at her handsome rescuer, she sensed he was a man worth waiting for; when Mark kissed her, she was truly caught—and he was enchanted by the magic in her sea-green eyes. Both had children they were raising alone, both had lost spouses to tragedy. Even at first meeting, however, Gillian and Mark felt an unspoken kinship . . . and a potent desire that produced fireworks, and dreams shared. Gillian wanted Mark's love, but could she trust Mark with the truth and shed her mermaid's costume for the sanctuary of his arms? The answer to that question is so touching, so loving that it will make you feel wonderful for a long time to come.

Do let us hear from you!

Warm regards,

Carolyn Nichols

Carolyn Nichols
Editor
LOVESWEPT
Bantam Books
666 Fifth Avenue
New York, NY 10103